Dead

Above

Ground

ALSO BY JERVEY TERVALON

Understand This

Living for the City

Dead

Jervey

Above

Tervalon

Ground

POCKET BOOKS
New York   London   Toronto   Sydney   Singapore

POCKET BOOKS, a division of Simon & Schuster Inc.
1230 Avenue of the Americas, New York, NY 10020

Copyright © 2000 by Jervey Tervalon

ISBN: 0-671-03468-5

First Pocket Books hardcover printing January 2000

10 9 8 7 6 5 4 3 2 1

Designed by Ruth Lee

Printed in the U.S.A.

For my parents:
Lolita Theresa Villavaso Tervalon and
Hillary Louis Tervalon

And my aunts:
Lucy Hazuier and Barbara Villavaso

Acknowledgments

I'd like to thank Tracy Sherrod, Joy Harris, Leslie Daniels, Oakley Hall, Max Schott, Blanche Richardson, Lance "LoveBug" Kaplan, Bob "B-Ball" Blaisdell, B. J. "Hardhitting" Robbins, Whitney Otto, Jonathan "Home-Slice" Gold, Charmaine Craig, Ellen Hazuier Distance, Geoffrey Middlebrook, and Alfred Bendixen for helping me along the way.

And a deafening shout of thanks to my two demanding G girls: Gina and Giselle.

New Orleans is situated in a delta, wherein the land has been created from flooding. . . . The combination of high rainfall and low altitude . . . poses a severe challenge to burial, and the Crescent City's inhabitants quickly discovered this dilemma. Imagine what would happen to buoyant, wooden caskets buried in the levee as the water table rose: A hard rain would push them back up above the ground.

—ROBERT FLORENCE, *City of the Dead*

New Orleans, 1946

I remember the day we were out on the porch at the old house fanning ourselves, hoping for a breeze. Mother saw Adele coming home to visit in that red dress so tight I don't know how she could have breathed, but she looked beautiful and she knew it. That dress, nothing she sewed with her own hands, had to be from Maison Blanche, and that fancy hat with a feather in the band covering her head full of sandy brown curls took the cake. Mother didn't wait for Adele to reach the top step before she grabbed hold of her.

"My, my, this is a surprise," Mother said.

Adele kissed her and then me. "I got more time to myself since Rene is away."

"Where to this time?" Mother asked.

Adele shook her head and smiled that coy smile of hers.

"Ding Bang . . . Sam Pang . . . someplace."

"But he's sending his checks home to you," Mother said.

"Oh, yeah. He keeps me happy," Adele said, pinching my shoulder hard.

"You quit that."

"I got to keep my little sister in line." Adele pinched me again.

Mother cut her eyes, and I knew better than to get Adele back.

"You come and stay with us," Mother said. "Rene's going to sea for what, six months? Time enough to be alone in that house."

"Oh, don't you worry. I'm keeping busy," Adele smiled like she does when she's getting away with something big. "You know Lucien Fauré?"

"Lucien Fauré?" The color washed right out of Mother's face.

Adele grinned.

"Are you crazy? Don't you know about that man!"

"I know he's some good-looking."

"Adele, he's the devil. He kills women."

Adele laughed. Mother didn't.

"Lucien kills women? Mother, I don't know who you've been listening to."

"Don't be stupid. You don't know that man."

People always talked about all the Irish in Mother;

how fair she looked and how when she got really mad she'd get almost as red as cooked crab. I guess since she was out of the house Adele could ignore that. She just kept laughing.

"Now, Lita, don't you think he's about the most handsome man you ever did see?"

I shrugged. If I said a word, I'd get the back of Mother's hand.

"Lucien's sweet as pie," Adele said, all innocent sounding, like she didn't know how angry she was making Mother.

Mother's hand flashed up, and I thought Adele was going to get slapped. Instead she flung the screen door open so hard it popped off its hinges and the door exploded shut behind it.

"Never saw her look so mad," Adele said.

I laughed. "Mother gets very mad."

"Maybe at you."

I thought Adele would just turn and walk down the steps and leave me to start dinner before Mother started shouting for me, but she lingered on the porch.

"She's wrong about Lucien?" I asked.

"She thinks she knows something about him, but those are just lies. He's so good to me."

"That's good," I said, but I couldn't help thinking about how right Mother was about everything except for Daddy.

"So when is she going to let you see somebody? You're seventeen."

I sighed.

"Ain't nobody I want to see."

"Girl, don't lie. You scared of her."

"I see boys," I said, halfheartedly.

Adele was right and I didn't feel like admitting it, so I kept my mouth shut.

"Sometimes you just have to do what you want. Can't always worry about every little thing," she said as she waved good-bye and headed up Gravier.

6

$\mathcal{M}$aybe Adele was even more glamorous in my eyes because she could get away with so much. I never understood why Mother tolerated her fast life; now that Adele was set with a hardworking husband, so pretty and dressed so fine, some people called her Little Lena Horne. Made it too easy for a man to fall in love with her. Adele saw Rene coming, she batted her long lashes and landed him easily. The idiot thought he caught himself the belle of the ball, but he was the one getting skinned, cleaned, and hung out to dry. What she saw in him was a colored man with a white man's job. Rene was so fair he couldn't work as a negro, but he found himself a position on a merchant marine ship, and that was it. Adele had schemed to get those fat paychecks and those frequent trips where Rene would be out at sea and she'd be alone and not have to answer to anyone.

Think she would have lived like a queen and made a few babies and spoiled herself rotten, but not Adele. Married, but with all that time and opportunity, she just chased men like a hungry dog looking for a bone.

Adele married Rene just when things were getting worse between Mother and Daddy, and because of that, Mother had only me to take out her troubles on. I didn't mind that she rode me like a French Quarter horse; she was much harder on herself than me. I'd see Mother waiting like a lovestruck girl at the kitchen table with Daddy's dinner warming on the stove, but he rarely made it home before we were all asleep. She had a broken heart and a sick heart and it was my job to keep it from getting worse. Maybe to keep him, Mother became pregnant, carrying twins she must have known she wouldn't see grow up. It was a miracle she survived to term. After they were born, it fell to me to raise them. By the time this Lucien business started, Ava and Ana were six years old, and they had long been my responsibility.

That was one bitter Monday: first the news of Adele's hot pants for Lucien, then Daddy coming home drunk, looking to beat somebody's behind.

In the darkness of the bedroom, a child on each arm cutting off my circulation, I was trying not to move, worrying I'd wake them and would have to get the girls asleep all over again. I needed to sleep myself, but I was too worn out, resentful at chasing my little sisters while Mother sat in the kitchen all Monday long brooding about Adele and wondering if Daddy would ever make it home for red beans and rice, his favorite meal. Daddy being gone was fine for me. At least the house was quiet.

Then he came stumbling in. I imagined Mother rushing to meet him, happy like Christmas in July. I heard them in the kitchen, Mother saying soothing words, Daddy grumbling.

"Bay, can I get you a cold drink? You don't want red beans and rice? You want me to cook a pork chop?"

I slid the sleeping twins from my arms and crept to the kitchen. There I saw Mother trying hard to light the stove.

"Woman! Are you some kind of fool!"

Daddy, dressed to the nines as usual for catting around, stood at the sink next to Mother, Mother still trying to strike a match.

"What? You got these damn matches wet! You dumb heifer!"

Daddy was a smallish man except for his arms from having to carry all that luggage in his Pullman porter days. He smacked Mother hard enough so that she bounced against the sink. He must have stunned her. She stood rigid and defenseless. Daddy grabbed her neck and forced her backward, turned on the faucet, and stuck her face under the stream of water. Clear as day I can still hear her gagging. He didn't stop. No, he kept it up till I thought she would die.

That was the first time I saw red. I mean really saw it, swam in it. I saw that bastard daddy of mine trying to kill Mother, and suddenly I was burning, raging in a sea of red hatred.

I rushed into the kitchen, startling the two of them, but still Daddy didn't let go. "You get out of here. Leave us be!" he commanded. He raised his hand like he could hit me although I was halfway across the room. He wanted me to run, but I didn't. No, that red rage propelled me to grab the big butcher knife from off the counter.

"Stop! I swear I'll cut you to hell!"

After a long moment of catching his breath from all that effort at trying to kill Mother, he laughed at me. I think he thought he could take the knife. His drunken ass stumbled toward me, hands reaching for the knife, and I cut him as easily as the chicken I cooked for dinner.

"Oh, God!" he shouted. "The little bitch cut me!"

"Get out!" I shouted.

"No, Lita!" Mother said, pulling me away, but I shook free and chased Daddy through the house and out the front door and into the street until I lost him in those tumbledown shotgun shacks around the corner.

I remember a full moon that night.

Daddy returned the next day with a bandaged hand. He didn't try to beat Mother, and he wouldn't look in my direction. Daddy knew I would kill him if he ever raised a hand to her again. This made me a woman in his eyes and in my own. In Mother's eyes I was the kind of woman who would never be beaten.

10

Daddy had some big secret. He wouldn't tell Mother what he was up to no matter how many times she asked. Men in dirty overalls came to work in the back-yard. They started digging and hammering and pouring concrete, but still Daddy wouldn't tell us what they were building. The frame of a small house went up, and I thought we were going to take in boarders. Only when they put in the counter and the stools did we fig-ure it out.

"A bar? What for?" I asked Mother.

"Your father says it's what we need to get ahead, and it's not a bad idea. We'll make this work."

I smirked, knowing the only getting ahead would be for Daddy, now that he could do his skirt-chasing and boozing right at home, but it wasn't my place to tell Mother. The bar was built quickly, and well enough; Mother saw to it that the builders didn't cut corners and pocket our money and make a laughing-stock of us.

I figured the bar would be closed in a few weeks or even sooner, but I was wrong. Mother knew how to make money, more money than Daddy could even lose or slip into his pocket. The first day we opened the doors, bums came in and rooted themselves on bar stools and didn't leave until we threw them out. I still wonder if they knew the kind of rotgut we were pouring. Daddy had the twins scrubbing labels off the cheapest beer he could find, then pasting on Falstaff or some other decent brand. Nobody complained. Those men just wanted some hole to climb in and some dirt to pull over themselves, and we had that hole and all the dirt they'd ever need.

11

*O*ne *evening before closing,* Adele came by. I was bone-tired, eyes stinging from all that smoke in the bar, wondering how I was going to make it to last call.

Late as it was, Adele looked like her evening just got started. She came over to me giggling like a school-girl. "He's here, Lita."

"Who's here?" Whoever it was, I didn't want them seeing me looking like what the cat drug in, with my hair under a scarf, stinking of spilled beer and smoke.

She wanted to point him out to me, but I inched backward, trying to catch Mother's eye. She was busy behind the counter, serving the last drinks and slipping the night's receipts, a wad of bills, deep into her bosom.

"Look, Adele's here," I said. Of course Mother brightened at the mention of Adele's name, but her mood turned sour as curdled milk when she spotted him in the crowded bar like she knew where he was to begin with. He smiled in our direction, and Mother dropped the bottle of beer she just opened.

"She brought that SOB to the bar!"

Adele waved to Mother and hurried over, beaming that smile. Mother yanked her close and shouted curses into her face. "Lucien! I thought you had sense enough to leave him be."

Adele looked shocked. "I thought if you met him, you'd see—"

Mother ripped off her apron and threw it into Adele's face, knocking her aside. Then she left the bar.

Adele looked confused, as though she didn't know whether to follow Mother or return to Lucien. Then he walked over. He stood looking at me with so much concentration it reminded me of how Mother balanced the books. I can't say I minded. I guess I didn't know what to expect, but he was beautiful, and I never felt that way about a man. Tall, over six feet and built like Joe Louis, and he wore his hair brushed back to show the waves of his curls. His eyes were pretty, but even smiling, his mouth was cruel.

"Lucien Fauré," he said, and held his hand out. I dried mine on my apron and reached for his, but instead he bowed his head and kissed my hand. "Enchanté." He ignored my embarrassment. "So," he said to Adele, "you haven't introduced me to your sister," in his deep, sweet voice.

Adele often forgot I was there. It was nothing that bothered me.

13

"This is my little sister, Lita Du Champ."

"Oh, you Du Champs have it all."

"Maybe some other Du Champs," I said.

"But look at this bar, and you have a motel and you had that fish market in the French Quarter."

"That's because Mother works like a dog for us to get ahead."

"Is that so?" Lucien glanced at Adele. "Now, your big sister here don't work, no? But she married a man with money. Isn't that a swell deal?"

I shrugged.

"Oh, please," Adele said, and rolled her eyes. Lucien saw her and flashed a frigid smile. She looked down at her hands like a little girl who didn't want a whipping.

"Where do you go to school when you're not working at this . . . bar?"

"Xavier Prep."

"Oh, really? You're a good girl. I like that."

Adele stood. "I'm ready to go."

"Sit down," he said flatly.

She did without a word against him.

"Well, Mademoiselle Du Champ, I will be seeing you again."

Adele smiled meekly as he led her out.

The next morning I was up as usual, running the girls' bath. No time to waste, because when I was through with them I had to help open the bar and somehow get to school on time so those damn nuns would stay off of my back. I lowered the squealing, protesting girls into the soapy water and turned to see Mother in the doorway.

"I cannot believe Adele," she said.

"Believe what about her?"

"You saw it!"

I knew she was talking about Lucien, but I didn't say anything.

"Why doesn't she just put a gun to her heart and pull the trigger?"

I waited for Mother to continue, but she shook her head and disappeared. The bathroom filled with the girls' laughter, but it didn't cheer me up. I knew Mother was working herself up to do something.

"Does she want to die?" Mother asked, more to herself than to me. She had returned with Ava and Ana's Sunday dresses.

I wanted to say, "She doesn't want to die. She

wants him because he's beautiful," but Mother didn't want to hear that.

"You want them to wear their Sunday dresses for playing in the backyard?" I asked.

"Don't talk nonsense. They're spending the day with Aunt Dot."

"Aunt Dot?"

"You heard me. Get them ready. Then we're going across town."

15

She didn't need to say it, it was obvious: no school for me today, and the bar wasn't opening for the early-morning drunks.

We walked the few blocks to Aunt Dot's small but pretty house. It was always freshly painted yellow, with pretty flowers growing in the yard, but I didn't like going there. Not only was Aunt Dot crazy, she didn't comb her hair. It just sat on her head like a big gray tumbleweed. She kept her house so clean her kids had to eat outside on the porch, and if they got dirty she'd scrub their skin until it was Indian-burn raw.

Mother didn't care for her sister. She wouldn't say it, but we all knew it, so I was surprised we were dropping the girls over there.

At the door Aunt Dot looked at us like we were strangers and shook her head when Mother asked her to watch the girls. Mother handed her the bag of groceries she had been carrying, then Aunt Dot invited us into the house.

"I'll watch them, but you better get back before they get hungry."

Mother cut her eyes at Dot but fished two quarters from her pocket and handed them to her. "Get them some milk and bread and butter."

"I'll make sure of that," Aunt Dot said, smirking.

Poor Ava and Ana hung onto each other as we walked out of the house.

"Where are we going?" I asked.

Mother just grunted and led the way to the streetcar, and from there we headed to downtown near the quarter where the Creoles lived. She stopped at a house that, though still attractive, had more than one broken window and a yard filling up with beer bottles and weeds. Mother gestured for me to stay on the sidewalk as she walked to the door alone. She knocked sharply and retreated to the street.

After a while the door opened and, bare-chested and unshaved, Lucien Fauré appeared. He squinted to see who had knocked, and when he recognized us he waved and stepped into the glare of hot morning sun. Somehow he looked more handsome than the night before, but still he had that vicious smile.

"Helen Du Champ," he said, in that rich voice of his that made me feel . . .

"Lucien! I have one thing to say to you. Leave my daughter be!"

"Well, ma'am, she's a grown woman. She can do what she pleases."

Mother gritted her teeth into a smile that was just as vicious as Lucien's. "She's a married woman."

"Really, now! Never would have guessed."

"Don't think you can play your tricks. If you lay your hands on her—" Mother didn't finish. She began to quiver and shake. I tried to lead her away, but I glanced back and saw Lucien on the steps smoking a cigarette and laughing at us.

"Better take care of that mother of yours. I don't believe she is long for this world."

Stupidly, I nodded. Then I shook my head and struggled to pull Mother on around the corner, wanting more than anything to get Lucien's eyes off of me.

Somehow I managed to walk Mother away with her leaning on me like a drunken man. I found a bench and some shade while we waited for the streetcar. I didn't know what to do, get Mother to the hospital or take her home, but home was a waste of time. Mother took herself to the hospital. Daddy wouldn't take her because he didn't give a damn. The streetcar arrived, and it was hell of crowded. I tried to struggle up the steps with Mother, but my grip slipped and she crushed me against the folding door.

"Yeah, get yourself on or off!" the bus driver yelled, and I felt the streetcar lurch forward.

"Wait, goddamn," I yelled, but it continued

rolling forward. Then I felt Mother being lifted off of me.

"Let me help you, ma'am," a man in an army uniform said. He helped Mother to a seat at the front of the streetcar. I was too tired to find a open seat in the back behind the colored sign, so I plopped down next to Mother. The GI looked down at me and smiled.

"Winston Michaels," he said, extending his hand for me to shake. He was a good-looking man even if he was slight, maybe five-seven and almost skinny. He had a olive complexion and the wavy hair of Creoles.

"Hey, coloreds in the back," the driver said.

"Mind your own business, bud!" this Winston said. "We got a sick woman here."

The driver turned to glare at us but didn't say another word.

"I didn't get your name," Winston said.

"Lita Du Champ, and this here is my mother, Helen Du Champ."

Winston nodded and reached to shake my hand, but the streetcar stopped abruptly, and he pitched forward almost into my lap.

"You'll need to change streetcars to get to Charity Hospital."

He pulled Mother up, and even though she was heavier and almost as tall as he was, he slid his arm around her and carried her to the exit well. The streetcar slowed to a stop, and I followed them off.

We weren't ten feet away when Mother started to come to.

"What the hell is going on here!" she demanded, pushing Winston away. Sputtering mad, she cocked her arm to hit him.

"Wait, Mother. He's a friend."

"A friend?"

"Winston Michaels, ma'am. Pleased to meet you."

Mother ignored him and turned to me. Now she had something else to be angry about. "And just who is this friend of yours?"

"Winston Michaels," he said, repeating himself. "Staff sergeant, U.S. Army."

"Good for you," Mother said, disdainfully. "And how did you meet this man?"

"Just now. On the streetcar."

"You're talking to strangers on the streetcar?"

"No, Mother. He helped me with you. You kind of fainted."

Mother paused, considering my words. "I do remember . . . ," she said, haltingly. Rivulets of sweat ran run down her face, and I thought she was going to faint again. Winston began fanning Mother, but her eyes rolled up into her head.

The streetcar wouldn't arrive for a while. Sitting out in the blazing sun, I was worried Mother might pass out again, but suddenly she shook her head and stood up like she wasn't ill at all and began walking in the direction of Aunt Dot's.

"Mother, you need to get to the hospital."

"Child, I'm not worrying with any doctors. I've got to pick up my girls."

I watched her swaying, unsteady walk, sure she wouldn't get far.

"I'd like to escort you. You might need help," Winston said, looking at me shyly, as though he expected me to say no.

I knew I needed help, any and all help. The closer we got, the weaker Mother looked, but she finished trudging to Aunt Dot's. There, Aunt Dot waved us in and turned her back to us and pointed to Ava and Ana, who were seated on the couch with their hands in their laps, like frightened rabbits.

"Those two are nothing but trouble! Had me hopping all day long. Next time I'm charging you."

Mother just shrugged. She was too busy gasping for air.

I worried she'd die right there. She looked so bad, the girls didn't run to her. They held onto my knees and watched Mother gasping in Aunt Dot's hot-ass parlor. Aunt Dot refused to open a window, and she had the single fan pointed at herself.

Winston leaned over to whisper to me, "We've got to get your mother to the doctor. She's getting worse. She looks like soldiers do when they're 'bout to drop from heat exhaustion."

I didn't reply. It wasn't heat. It was her heart.

"Aunt Dot, I need to get my mother to the hospital."

"Oh yes, she looks bad," Aunt Dot said, with all that fake sympathy dripping from her lips.

"Can you drive her?"

"Child, I want to, but my car ain't been running."

Winston jumped up. "I'll be right back," he said. For a small man he looked mighty big as he double-timed out of the house.

"What's all this commotion?" Mother asked, again awake.

21

"Oh, your Lita is all worried about you fainting."

"I told her not to bother."

Just then one of Aunt Dot's children came in, Richie, the big, quiet one.

"You!" Aunt Dot said.

The boy froze.

"Get out!"

"But Mama, I ain't been in the house all day."

"You heard me. Don't test my patience."

"Aw, Mama! I'm hungry."

Aunt Dot eyed him like a cat about to rip up a mouse. "Get my strap and lie across the bed."

Richie might have been hungry, but the mention of the strap broke him down to a sobbing eight-year-old. He returned with a cruel-looking belt and handed it to Aunt Dot, trembling and wailing, and walked to the bedroom unfastening his pants.

Aunt Dot smiled wickedly.

"Excuse me, I just need to take care of this bad boy."

After a long weary moment the girls had forced me down into a chair and hung onto my shoulders like desperate monkeys. We heard the first vicious stroke and then Richie's hysterical wails. Even Mother, who had a heavy hand, had to shake her head when the strokes and the wails continued. She pulled herself upright and wobbled to the bedroom. "That's enough. You gonna kill that boy!"

Through the open door we heard them arguing.

"Helen, you need to mind your own children," we heard Dot say, then we saw Richie running for his life through that parlor, one hand trying to hold up his pants to conceal his bloody cheeks.

Mother returned, looking disgusted. "What are you waiting for! Let's get the girls home," she said.

Ana and Ava moved almost as fast as Richie to clear out of the house.

"Mother," I said, trying to get her to slow down, "we should wait for Winston! He's gonna help us get to the hospital."

"Lita, I'm not worrying about some boy you just met to do for us."

I followed as she pulled the girls behind her. It was like her health had just snapped back. She had color, and she wasn't sweating bullets.

"Hey," I heard someone shout from the street. A beat-up station wagon pulled up alongside of us. Winston hung out of the window, waving.

"Surely that boy isn't following us," Mother said.

"He wants to drive us."

"Out of the question," Mother said, ignoring Winston and continuing her quick pace. It lasted less than a street length of me waving for Winston to follow as I tried to keep the girls in line. Mother fainted straight away, landing on a soft spot of very thick Saint Augustine grass. We gathered around, fanning her until Winston parked and carted her into the station wagon.

After the nurses wheeled Mother away I turned to the girls, who sat slumped together looking more scared than at Dot's. Maybe they could tell I was lying when I told them Mother would be all right.

"I need to get my sisters home. Thanks for all your help," I said to Winston. He nodded like he couldn't think of anything to say.

"I could drive you. I got the car til tomorrow."

"You've done too much —"

"It's no trouble at all."

He just wanted to see where I lived. I liked him well enough, but I didn't want him coming by wanting to court and maybe hounding me.

"Thank you, but no," I said.

Winston took it well enough and followed us out to the streetcar. We waited for what seemed like more than an hour.

"Maybe you missed the last one," Winston said.

"I don't think so," I said.

"Tell you what, if you're still here waiting by the time I pull the car around, let me give you a ride."

He straightened up behind the steering wheel and drove slowly around the corner. The streetcar was nowhere to be seen, and as tired as I was, I didn't want it to come. I wanted to ride home. When Winston reappeared, I was more anxious to get in than my sisters. The girls happily crawled into the backseat, so excited I had to smack their thighs to calm them down enough to give Winston directions. We drove there more slowly than he had to, because he kept trying to catch looks at me.

"This is it," I said, waving off his offer of help and carrying the girls, one in each arm, to the porch. I hoped Daddy would be gone, chasing skirts or whatever he did, but I saw the light on in the kitchen. I thought of sleeping with the girls in my broom closet of a room so I wouldn't have to walk by him on the way to theirs.

"Come here," I heard Daddy say. He was drunk again. I tucked the girls into bed and then came back to see what the bastard wanted.

He sat slumped at the wobbly kitchen table, a bottle of his own belly-rotting, cheap whiskey in front of him.

"Where's my money?" he mumbled.

"Money? I don't have no money for you."

Daddy looked up, focusing his bloodshot eyes on me.

"No, I guess you don't. People told me about you two not opening the bar."

"Mother got sick. She's at the hospital."

"Hell with that! Don't you ever close that bar. I don't care if somebody cut your damn head off!"

I tried to ignore him, but he wasn't having any of it, so I threw oil on the fire. "You're gonna have to work the bar yourself tomorrow. I'm going to be at the hospital."

Daddy turned and glared at me and pushed himself upright. "You think you're grown and you want to carry yourself like you the man of this house. Yes, you do. But they ain't but one man and you looking at him."

"That might be so, but I'm not working tomorrow."

"You little bitch," Daddy said, and made a move toward me. I was already at the knife drawer. Daddy backed up to the stove and grabbed a skillet.

We stood there waiting for the other to make a move.

"You just better be at that bar or you'll see."

"Go to hell," I said.

Daddy left, still carrying that skillet.

Early the next morning I tried to get the girls dressed and on to the hospital before Daddy came back from his tomcatting around. I tried not to let on to the girls how worried I was for Mother and how sorry I felt for myself, but I'm sure they suspected how bad she was. I knew I couldn't live with Daddy. I'd either kill him or he'd kill me. Working full-time at the bar would kill me or make me crazy. Mother had to live at least for another year. One more year to finish school, then if I had to take the girls, or come whatever, I could handle it. I heard somebody unlocking the door. Damn, I thought, Daddy's home. No, Mother came in, looking tired but not at death's door.

The girls rushed over and held on like they thought she might get away. Before I could get around to asking, Mother laid it all out. "There's nothing they can really do. I got what they call an enlarged heart. They gave me some pills and told me to take it easy." She laughed then, sounding girlish. "Now, that's something I know I won't be doing. None of it is gonna make much of a difference. I just feel bad for you girls."

"Don't say that."

"It's the truth," Mother said, and sat down and started to braid Ana's hair.

"Sometimes, Lita, I want to sleep forever."

"You just need some rest."

Mother sighed, and finished Ana's hair and waved Ava over. "I sure do. God knows I do."

Daddy was gone for the better part of a week. I heard rumors of someone seeing him in Baton Rouge, or maybe it was Houston. Anyway, at least for those few days

Mother got her rest, and I ran the bar on my own. I did hire a cousin to work days so I could continue school.

Cousin had a lame leg and was pretty slow-witted, but he was the most honest man I knew. Even so, Mother sent the girls down to the bar every couple of hours to collect money and spy on him.

It surprised me that Mother didn't mention Adele again. Adele had started all this nonsense, sending Mother into the street to fight to protect her, and the effort just about did her in. Those days of Mother being everything to us was over. She didn't have the strength to fight for herself, let alone for Adele. Adele was on her own.

I decided to marry this Winston soon as I knew for a fact he wasn't a drinker or a carouser or a sugar daddy. Once I knew he was nothing like my own father, then I knew I would do it. Winston wanted the wedding yesterday, but I told him he had to wait for an answer. I had just turned seventeen; he could wait a year. I didn't tell anyone that I was engaged to be engaged, because I didn't want anyone to tell me my mind. If I told Adele, she'd just say, "Girl, you copying me. Marrying your way out of the house to get out from under Mother." That was the difference between me and Adele; she didn't have a problem with Daddy. I had the problem with him. It wasn't that Daddy treated her better than me; he didn't. He wasn't heavy-handed with us as long as we did what he said. He mostly ignored us. He saved the beatings for Mother. But all the same I hated living under his roof. Adele couldn't live the way she wanted under Mother's roof even though Mother bent over backward to please her and let her get away with everything under the sun. I guess Mother knew that Adele couldn't help herself with men, and there wasn't much use fighting other than trying to keep her from bedding down with murderers.

See, with me Mother was different. She watched me like a hawk. If I stayed too late at school I'd get a beating. If I stayed too long at the movies she'd come looking for me. Maybe Mother needed me, and she didn't need Adele. She adored Adele but didn't expect much more from her than to dress pretty and wipe her own behind. Sometimes I suspected Mother was grooming me to take over all her problems once she was gone. Daddy, the girls, Adele—all of it. I wanted something else for myself.

The smell of catfish frying found my appetite before I saw Mother standing in front of the stove, cooking. Fridays she fried catfish for us and the barroom customers. From a big bucket on the floor Mother reached for a catfish and dipped it into milk, then rolled it in the cornmeal and slid the fish into a cast-iron skillet. The fish sizzled as it browned in the hot lard. Working fast and effortlessly, she cooked more than a dozen fish. She'd talk now—cooking relaxed her.

"Mother, how did you and Daddy meet?"

Mother looked up without pausing in the cooking of the catfish.

"Get down that big kettle, and I'm going to need more lard."

I did as she asked and then asked the question again.

"Why do you want to know?"

"Just curious."

"It's none of your business. . . ." Then Mother's expression softened. "He was working for somebody . . . and before I knew what was happening, he slipped me a ring. He was a charming man back then. I don't like to think about it because how much he's changed. Why are you so interested in marriage?"

I didn't know what to say. If I said another word, she'd know everything.

"I never heard . . . I mean, you never told me anything about it"

"We met. That's all you need to know."

I left the kitchen. I needed to know. I needed to know why she married a man like him. I didn't want the girls to make that mistake. I didn't want anyone to make that mistake.

"Lita!" Mother called, and I hurried to return to the steaming kitchen.

"Why are you so interested in my marriage?"

"Just curious."

"You've never been curious before."

"I guess I'm getting older."

Mother rolled her eyes. I turned to leave. "Stay," she said.

I did, but I couldn't bring myself to look into her eyes.

"This is about that man. That soldier who comes by to see you." I froze.

"He's courting you."

"Mother, what're you talking about?"

"You think maybe I married a man like this boy you like. You think Daddy started out churchgoing and hardworking and became lazy and good-for-nothing. Isn't that right?"

I nodded.

"Your father was never a choirboy, but neither was he a bad man. Life can surprise you. Sometimes in a good way, sometimes it drives you to your knees. You think you know what you're doing, then you find out you're wrong. Men get bored. That's how it is."

"Then what?"

"Then what?" Mother laughed. "What does anybody do? They play the hand they're dealt. You get by. You put up with it. That's all."

"Mother, I'm not engaged. We're just talking."

Even though the kitchen was sweltering and both

our faces were dotted with sweat, her eyes froze me like winter.

"Tell this Winston to bring himself over."

"Over?"

"You heard. Tell him to bring himself over so we can get this all out in the open."

"Get what in the open? I haven't given him an answer."

"Men take that for yes. I need to tell him a thing or two. Just so he knows the kind of woman I am."

I shook my head and began to cry. Usually Mother ignored tears, but not this time. She put down a catfish and patted my hand.

"Don't worry, Lita. I'm not going to chase your man away. I just want him to know what I expect. Because if he thinks he's some two-bit Romeo, he's got another thing coming."

"I'll tell him."

"You do that, girl."

I left the kitchen still crying.

Later that night in the bar Winston came by, pulling his hat low and the collar of his leather bomber jacket up, trying to look like a secret agent or something. Other than that streetcar ride when Mother was really sick, Winston tried to keep his distance from Mother. I was comfortable with that. Long as Mother wasn't

throwing knives, I could live with how they got along.
Now, though, she wanted him to come by, and it wasn't
for a pleasant chat. Mother only kissed one man's feet,
and that was Daddy. All others knew what she thought
of them, and most people had sense enough not to mess
with Helen Du Champ.

I waved Winston over as I washed beer glasses.
"We need to talk," I said.

He looked at me, all moony-eyed.

"Mother wants to talk to you."

"She does?" At first he looked a little nervous.
Mother liked doing that to people; keeping them fear-
ful. "She wants to talk about us. You told her?"

"I didn't tell her anything. She figured it out. That's
how she is," I said.

He pulled a comb from a pocket and began working his unruly hair into some kind of shape. Getting
himself ready for the big song-and-dance.

"You've got to tell her we're not ready. We're just
friends."

Shocked, he stopped combing his hair. "But we are
ready—maybe not this moment, but we're talking dates."

I shook my head. "Don't you do it! Don't you get
her thinking about me any more than she is."

"So what am I supposed to say? What's she's going
to say to me?"

I felt like throwing a beer bottle at him. "She's
going to grill you. She wants to know what, when, and
how and if we did and if I'm knocked up."

Now he looked as panicked as I felt.

"We haven't even been—she don't have a thing to be worried about."

"Well, you tell her that. Come on."

I took him by the hand and led him to the house. There, I called out for her. "Mother! Winston's here."

I knew she was probably in the kitchen getting Daddy's dinner ready that he was never home to eat. She stuck her head out and scowled at the two of us.

"Mother, this is Winston. You remember him?" I said as I led him into the kitchen. Mother sat at the kitchen table, shucking peas into a bowl.

"Pleased to meet you, ma'am," Winston said, extending his hand to Mother.

Mother looked at his hand until he just let it drop away. The soul-freezing scowl started to get to Winston. His eyes darted around the room, searching for some way to escape.

"What are your intentions?" Mother asked, pointing at a chair for him to sit in.

"Excuse me, ma'am. I don't think I heard you right."

Mother sighed and repeated the question.

"What are your intentions? Are you serious about my daughter?"

Like most people, Winston couldn't bring himself to look into Mother's eyes when she was in one of her no-nonsense moods.

"Well," he said. "We're just talking."

"I'm going to ask you again, do you have intentions?" she said. Her eyes paralyzed him, like he was a
frog staring at a flashlight.

"I mean, I'd like to, at some point."

"You'd like to what?"

A long moment passed. I don't think he took a
breath.

"Ma'am, at some point, I'd like your daughter . . ."
Winston paused and looked at me, his eyes begging for
me to do something, free him before Mother ate him
alive.

"Mother, we're only talking—"

Mother glanced my way, and I shut my mouth.
"I'm talking to the boy," she said, and returned her
attention to Winston.

"Ma'am, I'm getting to know your daughter."

"That's what I'm worried about."

"Ma'am, you don't have to worry about nothing
like that. I truly respect your daughter."

"I've heard that before. Men say all kinds of things
when they want something."

Winston shook his head. "No, ma'am. I just want
to get to know your daughter."

Mother scowled. "You want me to be happy about
that?"

"No—I'm trying to explain."

"We've gone over all that."

"Well . . ."

Mother shrugged. "Do you want to marry my daughter?" she asked.

Winston was done for. His shoulders sagged in defeat. "Yes, I want to marry her."

I cursed in front of Mother for the first time, but Mother must have not heard it, or she ignored me.

"That's it. Don't you feel better getting that off your chest?"

Winston looked exhausted but relieved. Mother smiled at the sight of busted-down Winston.

"So when are you two setting the date?" Mother asked him. Then she looked at me, but she wasn't mad. No, she was happy. She approved of Winston.

"Mother, we're not ready for that."

"I'll think of a date," Mother said.

"Mother—"

But there was no use. Mother had made her mind up.

We all walked back to the bar in silence, Winston and I trailing Mother. He wanted a sign from me that he had done okay, but I ignored him. I imagined my married life working as a barmaid, cooking dinner for Daddy, so busy taking care of the girls I wouldn't have time to start my own family. This Winston couldn't stand up to Mother, but why did I expect him to? Mother was Mother. If she only had a man one-tenth as smart and tough as she was, we'd own New Orleans.

The bar was more crowded than when we left it. Cousin was doing his best to handle the last-round drinkers, but he counted slowly and was probably giving too much booze and being paid too little for it. Mother rushed behind the cash register, and I started serving beers and whiskeys to the room full of lowlifes and drunks. Winston returned to his usual table near the zinc counter, where we could talk as I made drinks. He sat down and immediately bolted up and began searching for something.

"What's wrong?" I asked.

He shrugged and continuing searching, stooping, looking beneath tables. Then I realized his leather jacket was missing.

"Where's your jacket?"

"I don't know. I thought I left it here on the back of this chair." He shook his head bitterly. "I should have taken it with me."

"Don't worry, we'll find it," I said.

I told him to wait, and as I made my round of the bar I checked out all of the tables and chairs, but it was too dark to see anything very clearly.

I felt rotten. He loved that jacket.

Mother saw me wandering around the room with an empty tray. She waved me over. "What are you, sleepwalking?"

"Winston's jacket disappeared."

"You mean somebody stole it."

Mother straightened her apron, stood up on a chair, looked out at the bar, and shouted so loud that glasses dropped and smashed on the hard floor. "Look here! Some son of a bitch stole my son-in-law's jacket. I want it returned, no ifs ands or buts, and I want it returned now! You got until we close. That's it. That's all I'm saying about the subject." Before Mother stepped down, she glared out at the drunks and drinkers, like an Amazon about to run some men through.

Embarrassed, Winston slunk low into the seat, probably trying to slide under that table.

Mother left the bar. Her job was over, and now everybody would see if she still could command respect. I had no doubt that even with a sick heart she could hold her own. Maybe ten minutes later, Cousin came up to me holding Winston's jacket. "Where'd you find it?" I asked.

"On the back of a chair. Like it had been there all night."

"Somebody didn't want to meet their maker," I said, and handed the jacket to Winston. He looked at it and shook his head.

"How'd—she'd know—?" Winston asked.

"She didn't know, but somebody did. Word would get back to her, and then she'd get a pound of flesh."

Winston shook his head. I knew he was thinking what kind of family he was marrying into.

"Listen, Winston. You don't have to. I mean, Mother is pushing me, but you really don't have to."

"I don't mind," he said.

*A*lmost immediately, Mother started planning for the wedding. She wanted just the right material for my wedding dress, so we caught the streetcar down to the Vieux Carré to a fabric shop. Negroes weren't allowed in the French Quarter, and normally Mother wouldn't go places where you couldn't go as colored, but in this case she was willing to pass. Mother could pass every day of the week if she wanted. She could break bread with the Klan, and they would gladly pass the butter. Adele wanted to come along with us, but she was a shade browner than me and Mother. That was just asking for trouble. Plus, mad as Mother was at her, it was the best thing all around that she gave up on the idea.

The shop was near Jackson Square, in one of those narrow alleys that smelled of stale piss. The windows of the shop hadn't been cleaned in who knew how long; dead flies and bugs cluttered the corners. We opened the door, heard a bell ring faintly, and entered a dark, cool room. A lady as old as I've ever seen came from behind a curtain and took a long look at us.

"I'm looking for French lace," Mother said, with a

expressionless face. The lady continued to look us over, then she finally turned and shuffled off to the rear of the store and began searching through a wall of shelves, looking at big swatches of material where the poor light was at its dimmest. I thought she would have to look forever to find anything, but she returned quickly with a fat roll of material.

"This for her?" the old lady asked.

Mother nodded. The old lady gestured for us to feel the material. Mother bunched some of it between her fingers. It was beautiful.

"Petite as she is, you'll not be needing more than a bolt and a half."

"How much for that?"

"Ten dollars?"

"Eight," Mother replied.

The old lady nodded, and we watched as the woman cut the material with a pair of scissors so large she barely could hold them in her hand. Then she wrapped the lace in butcher paper and stuffed that into a bag.

"You don't even want to sweat on material that fine, no. You gonna make one beautiful bride."

"The girls at Xavier Prep are going to be jealous," I said to Mother in a low voice.

The old woman raised an eye brow and muttered, "Passe blanche."

Mother shrugged. I had given it away, mentioned my colored school.

The old woman laughed with her mouth all wide like a damn white crow. "I'm too old to care about that," she said.

Mother didn't blink. She paid for the lace and we left. She tried to keep from exploding, but her face got even redder. "That's why I don't like to have nothing to do with them. Too hard to keep civil." I didn't know what to say. Mother didn't talk much about them. "They value their white skin so much because deep down inside they know it don't mean a damn thing. Trash is trash."

40

Without a doubt Aunt Dot was the best seamstress in New Orleans. Even with her evil, crazy ways she had far more work than she could ever do. Everyone came with magazines showing the new styles, and Aunt Dot would do them better and charge many a pretty penny. Cutthroat as she was, she made such a good living she could afford a nice home, even if it was a little on the small size, and she didn't even need to have her husband—a man she terrorized as much as Daddy terrorized Mother—do anything but run errands for her.

Rich white folks paid a price for dealing with Aunt Dot. I heard if they did anything but kiss her behind, she'd tell them to hit the road. So they smiled and paid and tried to stay on her good side, if they could find it.

I didn't want Mother to have to put up with all that nonsense because of me. "We don't really have to get Aunt Dot to do it. We can find somebody else who could do the job," I said to Mother as we rode the near-empty streetcar back home.

Mother rolled her eyes at my suggestion "The ones who can hold a candle to her we can't afford. You are going to have the best dress money can buy. I'm just going to have to bite my tongue with that woman."

We arrived to Aunt Dot's just when a midday shower broke. We ran to the porch and saw that poor little Richie sitting on the steps, getting soaked to the bone.

"What are you doing out in the rain?" Mother asked, but even with the water running down his face, we could see that he had been crying.

"She mad at me for eating all the bacon," he said in a gasping voice.

Mother squatted down in front of him. The boy had fresh welts on his legs like tiger stripes.

"You just got a beating?"

"Oh, yeah. And when I go in, she gonna beat me some more."

"No, she's not," Mother said, and lifted the boy up and ushered him to the door. Mother knocked, and as we waited Richie held onto Mother's leg like it was the only thing that could save him.

The door flung so hard it slammed against the wall on the other side and almost rebounded shut. There was Aunt Dot looking like a crazy witch with her tumbleweed hair looking crazier than usual, and for good effect she had a razor strap in her hand.

"Dot," Mother said, and stepped forward, driving Aunt Dot back into the parlor.

"That boy is on my last nerve. He's got some beating coming soon as company leaves," Aunt Dot said, waving that brutal razor strap at him.

Richie began to wail. Mother shushed him.

"Listen," she said to Richie, "you want to come spend some time at your Aunt Helen's?"

"Who's she?"

"Me," Mother said, laughing.

"Yeah," the boy said.

Aunt Dot frowned.

"I can't believe you came all the way over here for that little troublemaker."

Mother looked up at her with so much scorn in her eyes I felt humiliated for Aunt Dot.

"What is it then?" she said, talking like she wanted us out of her nightmare hair.

Mother thrust the grocery bag with the french lace into her hands. "You niece is getting married. The wedding's a little ways off, so you have all the time you need to get the dress together."

"Who, Lita?" I smiled stiffly. "Hope you marrying somebody with money. Somebody like Adele's Rene. That girl got it made."

Mother's scowl got even deeper.

"You know she still comes to see me. She told me about that Lucien. That daughter of yours got a wild hair. What you gonna do with her?"

Mother had to bite her lip to keep her mouth shut. I thought she would draw blood. "We've got to go now," she said.

Now Aunt Dot looked like she was ready to scream. "You don't expect me to do this for free. I'm the sole support for five big-eating boys."

"Well, I'll be taking this one off your hands."

Aunt Dot rolled her eyes. "Irregardless, I need to earn a living."

"Regardless. The word is 'regardless.'"

Aunt Dot rolled her eyes at Mother's correction.

"How much?" Mother asked.

"One hundred dollars."

Mother gasped. "Fifty," she managed to say.

"Seventy-five," Dot said.

"Fifty."

Aunt Dot paused and chewed over the numbers.

"Alright. Since we are family and Lita is my niece I'll do it."

"That's mighty white of you," Mother said.

"And if you take the boy."

"I'll take the boy."

Mother handed Aunt Dot some balled-up bills, grabbed the boy by the hand, and we were outside so fast, walking away up the street, I hardly noticed the downpour until I was soaked.

We arrived home with another mouth to feed and for me to look after, and while I dreaded the extra work and responsibility I was glad Mother did what she had. Aunt Dot hated Richie and had it out for him, her own little boy. She was one crazy bitch.

The girls, Ava and Ana, were in the yard jumping rope when they saw Richie. Both of them stopped dead and gave him a looking-over.

"Your cousin is going to be staying with us for a little bit," Mother said.

Ana smiled at him, but Ava frowned. They were twins only in appearance; sometimes the only thing the two of them seemed to have in common was their love of each other's company. They made quite a contrast, Richie's handsome features and brown skin next to the girls' near-white skin and their reddish brown mops of hair. Richie was bigger than the both of them, and I kind of worried he might bully them, but soon after we left them in the yard to play, Richie came running into the barroom, crying.

"What's wrong?" Mother asked.

The boy stood there rubbing his eyes, red faced. "Those girls beat me up."

It took Mother's heavy hand to straighten that nonsense out.

44

The wedding plans moved full steam ahead, but I was plain overwhelmed with school and the kids and everything else, so I just followed Mother's lead. She knew everything that needed to be done, and even though her heart was weak she worked so hard scheming and plotting, she made me tired.

The truth was, whatever doubts I might have had at first had been replaced with the knowledge that my life would change. I could hardly wait to move in with Winston, and even though Mother wasn't crazy about him, she wanted this for me. It wasn't something I expected from her. Mother even started asking my opinions about things—what did I want served? How many people to invite? Did I want my school friends to receive invitations? Mother seemed to do well under all the new work she had given herself.

Then Adele showed up. I was in the parlor looking over the books for Mother when I heard a knock at the door. Before I had it open wide enough for someone to enter, Adele pushed her way inside. She wore a flowery dress and straw hat that looked as cheerful as Adele was sad. Her eyes were red, her face tearstained, and she carried a handkerchief she dabbed at her face.

"What's wrong?" I asked.

"You set a date, and you didn't tell me a thing! I'm your sister!"

"I thought Mother would have told you."

Adele sneered. "Mother hasn't said a word to me since I told her about Lucien."

That surprised me. Usually those two talked at least a couple times a week, and if they argued they'd have it worked out sooner than later.

"She's at the bar. Go talk to her."

"No, she doesn't respect me. If I leave Rene for Lucien, she'll never talk to me. I'll be dead to her."

"You're going to leave Rene?"

Adele turned away. "I haven't talked to him about it."

"Don't jump the gun. Think about what you're doing."

Adele pulled the straw hat off, and as if on cue, the waterworks began. Adele could turn it on in a wink. I held on to her till she pulled herself together enough so that we could talk.

"Adele . . . what do you want me to do?"

"Make Mother speak to me. You can do that."

"I'll ask her."

"Am I going to stand in your wedding?"

"I thought you were."

Adele calmed herself. She opened her purse and retrieved a compact and examined her face. "I thought you didn't want anything to do with me either," she said, looking at her lips in the round compact mirror as she put on fresh lipstick.

"Adele, you're my big sister. I wouldn't do that to you."

Adele smiled for the first time. Already she looked

back to normal, beautiful and without a care in the world. "I'm going to talk to Mother. I think we should talk." Adele closed her compact and straightened her dress and walked on to the house. Almost immediately I knew it was a mistake. Mother wasn't going to give in to Adele's view of things. Maybe Adele had a reason to be confused. Her other flings didn't outrage Mother, but she knew Mother well enough to know that once she had made up her mind about something important, nothing was going to change it. And I guess it wasn't surprising that she felt the need to try. Adele needed Mother in a way that even the twins didn't. She wanted Mother to approve of her, and to accept whatever crazy mess she got herself into. I felt sorry for Adele, and that made me feel bad. It was easier to envy her or be mad at how easy she got along with Mother or how easy it was for her to find a good husband.

Even though I had my head in the icebox stacking beer cases, I heard sharp steps heading my way. I turned to see Adele hatless and crying, hand cupping her cheek.

"What happened?"

"Mother slapped me!"

I wanted to say, "bout time," but I didn't.

"I can't let Lucien see me like this."

I took one of the cold beers in the back of the icebox and handed it to her. She seemed to calm down a bit when the cold bottle touched her skin.

"What happened?" I asked again.

"I told Mother my plans, and she slapped me."

"What did you tell her?"

Adele sighed. "I said I was thinking about leaving Rene."

"What did she say?"

Adele laughed a hard, short laugh. "She didn't say a thing. She just stood up and slapped me to the ground, yeah."

I shook my head. "Adele, do you know what you're doing?"

"How could you ask me that? Here you are planning to marry. I just want the same thing. I want to be happy and to be with the man I love."

"Guess you know what you're doing."

Adele didn't bother to answer. She just turned her back to me and walked out.

Mother didn't speak about the fight with Adele, and I didn't have the courage or the stupidity to bring it up. Mother hardly drank, but she found the whiskey and sank into a glowering, smoldering funk. Even Daddy had sense enough to give her plenty of room and for once cooked a meal for himself. One Sunday evening after the barroom closed and the family was waiting for dinner, I learned how much she hurt. She pulled Daddy aside, who surprisingly enough was still around the house five minutes after the sun had set. Usually by then he was gone like a ghost. I overheard their conversation in the hallway as I tended to the twins and Richie.

"Can't you do something?" Mother implored.

Those were strange words, coming from her. She hardly asked Daddy for anything—she was too busy taking care of his every need.

"I said I'd talk to him," Daddy responded, as though he meant it.

49

"You're going to have to do more than talk to him," Mother said, urgently.

A long pause. "You mean you want to find some-body to take care of him?"

"I'llpayforit. Justfindsomebody," Mother said, the words running together.

Daddy shook his head. "You're talking about Lucien Fauré. You just don't go out of your way to mess with him."

"That's your daughter you're talking about. Some-thing has to be done. Even if I've got to do this myself."

"Look, if he lays a hand on her, I'll be over there with a bat to beat his ass, but I'm not going to risk my life because Adele got hot pants."

Mother returned to the dining room carrying a tray of uncooked chicken. "Oh God," she said, "I forgot to cook the chicken."

That was Mother's life back then: planning one daughter's wedding, while plotting to kill her other daughter's lover.

Mother even talked Daddy into leaving his gun home for her. That made me worry that sooner or later she would slip out and visit Lucien and put a bullet into his head. She said she wanted her own, but Daddy was too cheap to buy one for her.

"Woman, we can share it. Ain't nobody stupid enough to come over here and try and rob the bar. They know me and they know I'm not a man to be messed with."

What everybody knew is, Mother paid the cops above and beyond the call of duty. Plus, they liked her and the fact that she poured them the good booze and not the rotgut Daddy insisted on serving. So Mother and Daddy took to sharing a gun. Most days he left it in the high cabinet, and most nights he took it with him. I'm sure the reason he didn't buy her her own is that sooner or later he knew she would get around to shooting him.

If Mother planned on killing Lucien, she'd have to do it in the early afternoon, because Daddy didn't get home from skirt chasing till late morning. And even if Daddy made it home at a reasonable hour, who'd watch the girls? I'd have to work the bar. As the weeks passed, the killer started to diminish in Mother's eyes. She became more interested in the wedding than plotting death.

I was sitting at the kitchen table near the fan enjoying the cool air as I wrote out wedding invitations when Richie burst through the door like his crazy mother was chasing him. It took a minute for him to catch his breath, then he gestured in the direction of the bar. "Some white man's in the bar crying his head off. He says he want to see you."

Some liquor salesman, sauced and down on his luck, I thought as I hurried into the near-empty bar-room—it was still a little early for serious drinking—and saw a man in a oversize suit at the counter, head in hands, sobbing like I've seen very few men do. Cousin didn't seem to have a clue of what to do with him. He looked relieved when he saw me tap on the guy's shoulder.

The white man glanced back and saw me.

He wasn't white. It was Rene Williams, my brother-in-law.

It took a minute for him to recognize me.

"Lita, have you seen her?"

"Adele? Not lately."

Rene had some kind of sailor outfit on that was at least a size too big. He must have just returned home from the ship. Even though I stood in their wedding and had gotten to know him well enough, it was surprising how white he was; straight dark hair, blue eyes, and pinkish skin.

"Changed the locks. I come home and the locks are

changed. I thought maybe I was at the wrong address because I've been out at sea so long. But I wasn't wrong. I paid for that house and I can't even go inside and take a piss. Excuse my French."

"The locks?"

I probably looked as alarmed as he was because he started to rifle through his pockets searching for something. A fat roll of bills fell to the floor, and he was so drunk I don't think he noticed. I picked it up and handed it to him. He thanked me and stuffed the roll into his pocket in such a half-assed fashion I was sure it would fall out again.

"You know, I came home expecting a juicy steak and a beautiful wife waiting for me, but what I get is a dead house with locked doors I don't have the key for." He eyed me suspiciously. "She's got another man? Is she screwing somebody?"

He was stinking drunk. One thing about Rene, he was usually a polite man, but he couldn't hold his liquor.

After he said the words, he realized what he had done and flushed pink. "I got to find her! You know something . . . please, I'm desperate here."

Rene stood up so abruptly he knocked the bar stool over. He wobbled dangerously as he bent to pick it up.

"I wish I could help you, but she hasn't been around."

Then with his blue, bloodshot eyes staring at me, jaw rigid and hands clenched, he asked in the voice of a confused, grieving child, "I want to see Helen. Call her out here."

Mother was resting, and I didn't want to disturb her, but I didn't think Rene would take no for an answer. He began to cry again, and I patted him on the shoulder. "Wait, let me see if she's awake."

Rene nodded, and I hurried into the house. Mother was awake, sitting up in bed, propped on pillows, writing something. Sometimes she wrote songs, poems, usually about Daddy. One song, "My Street Angel," was for him. Daddy was street, but he was no angel.

Mother didn't look well, pale and sweating as though writing were too much exertion for her.

"Mother, Rene's here."

She sighed deeply. "I was wondering when he would get back."

"He's drunk and crying."

"What, Adele's left him?" Mother sounded as though she expected the news.

"She's changed the locks."

"Changed the locks?" Mother slowly shook her head. "Get those pills off the dresser for me and a glass of water."

I did as she asked. It took some effort for her to swallow the pills; those three fat, yellow pills.

"She done left him for Lucien. She's my daughter, but damn if I know what she thinks."

"He wants to talk to you."

"I expect he would."

Mother waved me over to help her dress. She looked so weak; strength would just leave her. It took a while to get her presentable, stopping often to let her catch her breath. She needed to lean on me as I led her to the barroom. Rene was still at the bar, slumped over like he had passed out. I hoped he had, because Mother would give it to him straight, and I wasn't sure he could handle that.

Mother was winded before we reached him, so she slid into a chair and gestured for me to shake him.

I did. He woke abruptly and panicked. I fell back almost into Mother's lap.

"You!" he shouted, pointing accusingly at me. His eyes seemed to look through me as he stepped forward, jabbing his finger near my face. "Lock me out my own house and expect me to stand for it!"

"Listen, Rene . . . ," Mother said, but her voice trailed off, and I don't think he heard her.

He grabbed me around the neck and began to shake me so hard I was lifted off the ground. Cousin limped out from behind the bar with the baseball bat in hand, and just as he swung, Mother shouted, "Rene, that ain't Adele!"

Rene stood there like he had been hit with cold water. He stepped back away from me, nodded to Mother, collapsed at a table, and began crying all over again.

Mother stood, shaking off whatever fatigued her,

and pulled up a chair alongside of him. "Listen, Rene. Leave her be."

"What?" he said, suddenly alert.

"She's lost to you. She's lost to me."

"What are you saying?"

"I'm telling you, she's . . ."

Mother couldn't finished the sentence. From where I stood, she shook with either rage or grief.

"Rene," I said.

He looked at me, and for a moment I knew he saw Adele in me again.

"Rene," I said, more firmly. "Do you know Lucien?"

"Lucien Fauré?"

"Yes," I said.

Color drained from his face. The poor man's white skin looked even whiter. He stood up and walked around crazily, kicking chairs aside and sobbing. Finally he returned to us and fixed his eyes on Mother. "Why didn't you stop her?" he said, in a more reasonable voice than I expected.

Again, Mother couldn't find the words.

"She did," I said. "She told Adele not to. That's why she hasn't been around."

Rene sat heavily into a chair.

"Just leave, Rene. Lucien changed those locks to show you what's his."

"But it's mine. I paid for that house with my own hard-earned money. Stuck out at sea with a bunch of goddamn rednecks, pretending I'm one of them. Then I come home to this. Where does he live? I'm going to settle this now."

Mother reached for the pencil behind her ear and scribbled the address for Rene and handed it to him. He turned to leave, but Mother stopped him with three words.

"He'll kill you."

"Oh, no—I'm gonna be the one who does the killing."

"Yes, then you'll be in Angola for the rest of your life, or maybe you'll get the rope."

Rene started for the door again but then stopped suddenly. "What would you do?"

Mother walked slowly over to him. "Listen, Rene. You're a good man. Truly, you deserve better than what my daughter's done to you, but she's ruined her life. If you tangle with this Lucien, you're either going to ruin your own or die. Bad men kill good men. Bad men kill bad men, but good men don't kill bad men. Walk away. I'm going to do the best I can to take care of her."

Rene headed for the door again, but then he stopped.

"You don't think I'm a coward?"

"No. I think you're a good man."

Rene finally walked out of the door.

Mother's head sank to her chest, and I helped her back to the bedroom. On the way she said, more to herself than to me, "God help him."

"You think he's going over there?"

"I gave him an address as far away from Lucien's as I could think of. Lucien would slaughter him like a lamb."

Most days Mother rested. She'd lie in bed too tired to read or anything else, but she always seemed to find some strength to quiz me about the progress of the wedding.

"What about those bridesmaids—have they been fitted yet?" Mother asked, trying to pull herself up.

"Yes, Mother. They've all gone over to Aunt Dot's."

"She give them some hell?"

"She made them pay up front before she'd even take a measurement."

"That woman is sick, but she better have those dresses done on time, or I'm going to have to see to her."

I nodded. The wedding kept her going.

"The church?"

"I've been checking every week. It's set. Father Fitzpatrick said he's looking forward to it," I said.

The wedding was nearing. I hoped Mother would hang on until then. In a way I began to dread my wedding. I suspected soon as the priest pronounced us husband and wife, Mother would drop dead.

Every so often she felt good enough to walk the girls and Richie to the sweet shop to buy them a treat. The girls as usual were too involved with themselves and their own plans and ideas and didn't seem to think much of Mother's illness. Richie, though, hung around Mother like an old dog. He would actually sit at the foot of her bed, listening to her breathe as she slept. While he was just a little older than the girls, he sensed the seriousness of the situation. I guess he had to. The girls had me to look after them, while Richie knew his only angel was Mother. Mother had brought him to a home where he was fed, and could come into the house like any other boy and not have to stay out in the rain waiting for somebody to throw him a nickel. And for the most he didn't have to fear being whipped and beaten bloody for nothing.

I'd try to think of some way to put his mind at ease, but I don't think he ever heard me.

"Nobody done nothing nice for me except for Aunt Helen."

If she started coughing or needed something he couldn't take care of, he'd drag me away from whatever I was doing. "She needs you!" he'd say, and pull with all the strength of his eight-year-old body. And if I moved too slow for him, he'd haul off and kick or scratch me to get my attention. I worried about that boy. There was something really sweet about him, but Aunt Dot had whipped him so, he had a wildness in his eye. At first I thought he might be trouble for Ava and

Ana, but then it turned out together they were too much for him. Once over a game of jacks he pounded Ana in the back so hard she couldn't catch her breath for minutes. Ava came at him with one of Mother's heels and busted his nose some good. So for a while he kept his distance from the girls.

I always trusted Mother's judgment, but after she took in Little Richie and turned her back on Adele, maybe her illness made it hard for her to think straight. I didn't want to tell her about Adele because I knew there would be yelling and carrying on. It was my choice. I had promised Adele she would be a bridesmaid, and I wasn't going back on it. I headed into her bedroom feeling like I was walking my last mile.

"Listen, if Adele comes, don't you expect me to be there."

"What?"

"You heard me. I will not attend a wedding with Adele."

"Mother!" I yelled so loud Daddy shouted, "What's going on in there?" from the kitchen.

"You're not being right; making me choose between the two of you."

"Then don't, but don't expect me to be there if Adele's in the church."

"You just totally cut Adele off and you brought that little boy in to replace her. Adele might do stupid things, but she's my sister."

Mother did her best to push up and out of the bed,

and probably if she had enough strength, she would have slapped me, but all she could manage was to sit up and glare.

"Adele made her bed, now she's got to sleep in it. There's nothing you or I can do to change it. It's up to her. But it's up to you to uninvite her if you want to see me there on your wedding day."

I didn't have anything to say. She had made her point. To try and get her to see mine would have been stupid. She was just being cruel. Toss Adele out of the family, and then the only person she'd have to turn to was this Lucien. Mother must have seen that. Family is what she lived for, so why would she deny that to Adele? Sooner or later Adele would leave him, and then where would she be? Alone. Mother could accept that, but I couldn't. There were many things I put up with from Mother—her temper, her heavy hand, being stricter than she had any need to be—because I thought she loved us and would do anything for us. I didn't have much fear growing up of anyone hurting us. I didn't need to fear anybody except for Mother, because Mother was our lioness, and she'd die protecting us. Sooner or later she would want us all back together again.

$\mathcal{S}$oon as Sheila, the bigmouth heifer yell-queen, finished chewing me out because I didn't show enough spirit, cheerleading practice was over. I didn't argue. I had too much on my mind to pretend I had any spirit to give. I would have quit if that wouldn't have been more trouble than not. I changed into my pleated skirt, which Mother hated me to wear because it was tight like the dresses Adele wore, but since she was in bed she didn't get the opportunity to see me pack it away in my bag. I also wore the sweater Winston had given me as a Valentine gift. He said I looked like Lana Turner in it, and of course Mother hated it. Usually to school I wore my hair in a ponytail because color-struck girls weren't likely to say something stupid under their breath like, "Oh, I heard she's trying to pass now," or "So, she has good hair. She's still not really Creole." Today I wore my hair down, and because of all the sun I had been getting cheerleading, my hair looked even lighter. I was going to the Vieux Carré, and to do that you had to pass. Colored weren't welcome except to work.

Practice ran late, and I was already close to the time I needed to be there, all the way on the other side of town. Then I saw Winston, waiting like he was at parade rest to escort me home. Well, the proof is in the pudding. He was going to have his way and walk me home from Xavier Prep even after I told him I didn't have time for him today.

"My, you look beautiful today. Really decked out," he said, giving me the once-over.

"Thank you," I said, hoping he noticed I didn't look happy to see him. Most days I looked forward to him carrying my books and buying me a malted on the way home, but now wasn't the time, and he had to go.

"I'm not going home," I said.

"Huh," he said, too busy checking out my legs to hear my words.

"I've got to run some errands for Mother."

"Sure, that sounds good. I don't have to be at the post office for another couple of hours."

"No, don't you worry yourself on my account," I said.

Finally the words got through his thick head: I wanted him to leave. He looked a little confused. I kissed him right there on the sidewalk in front of the school, something that could get me in trouble and something he thought was improper, but he stood there stunned as I walked quickly away. I knew he'd follow, so when I got around the corner I ran back into the school and waited long enough that I was sure he wouldn't be there. But he still was, standing there at the edge of the sidewalk, being a soldier. I had to walk all the way around the schoolyard to avoid him. Even though school had let out more than a hour ago, enough girls were lingering around, flirting with boys and carrying on. Off-campus I walked in the wrong direction, hoping Winston would have given up by now. I arrived at the streetcar to the Vieux Carré. The driver looked like nothing but trouble—fat face, red neck—but he barely looked at me as I dropped my money into his hand.

"Good afternoon, miss," he said, in a rusty voice.

I nodded and sat up front in the white section. I didn't feel uncomfortable, because I knew I fit in. That wasn't the problem. The only thing that could cause a headache is if somebody I knew got on. There would be that awkward moment when they'd see me and wonder what was I up to. They'd think I was intending on jumping ship and trying to pass. I didn't give a damn about looking white. I would have been a lot happier if I was Adele's shade, where passing wasn't so easy an option. Darker people sometimes judged me as if I was proud to be near-white. Mother raised us to be what we were — colored and proud, never wanting to be something we weren't. Whites wanted us to believe they were pure and those of us colored who looked like them were closer to being pure, but I didn't believe it. They were no different from us. As long as we wanted their purity, we would be less than they were, even if we were as white as snow. I didn't want it, and because of that I knew I was their equal.

The streetcar stopped near to the river on Canal, and I walked the mile to Jackson Square. It felt good to be walking. Spring was about the only time of year you could without sweating like a pig. The Quarter was crazy even in the late afternoon. Some sailors stumbled toward me, drunk as skunks, leering until I took my heel off and showed them that I meant business. Yeah, the Quarter was genteel and ritzy and Jim

Crowed, but it was also sailors looking for prostitutes or facedown in the street, drunk.

At the Café du Monde I found a seat near the water fountain facing Jackson Square and away from most of the crowd eating beignets and trying not to get too much powdered sugar on their clothes. I loved those beignets myself, but I needed to lose ten pounds before the wedding. Also, I didn't want to get caught stuffing my face when he walked up.

I ordered a coffee and waited and watched people passing by. It didn't take long for another idiot to hit on me.

"Say there, miss, do you need some company?" this potbellied redneck said.

"I'm waiting on my husband."

He winked. "Lady, look, if you worried about whether or not I can afford you —" The fat man slipped a roll of bills from his dungarees. "I like to tip. I surely do."

This time he winked twice. Right as I was getting ready to retreat to another table, I looked up and saw Joe La Piccolo standing behind him. He turned and saw Joe's New Orleans Police Department uniform.

"Hello, there," the fat man said, nervously.

"Hello there, my ass! Are you trying to make time with my girl?"

The fat man shrank in size. He looked like a scared little kid when Joe pulled his billy club out and spun it slowly.

"No, sir!"

"Well, you better be on your way," Joe said, and as the man turned to leave, Joe's billy club darted out and clipped his wrist. The fat man yelped and hightailed it across the street.

Joe turned to me, grinning. "Lita! Yeah, it's some good to see you." He swung his legs across the iron-work surrounding the café and hugged me. "Man, so I heard you gonna do that thing and tie the knot?"

I nodded. Joe shook his head in fake disbelief. We once went out behind his father's back and my mother's. Joe's father was mobbed up and controlled the jukeboxes in the Ninth Ward. I met Joe because he collected for his dad while still in uniform. I didn't try to hide I was colored, but he had a thing for me in a bad way. Kept coming around the bar chasing off customers until I consented to have a Coke with him. I didn't know what to expect, but Joe was a gentleman, a real sweet man. Drove me across the Lake to a nice little restaurant and told me how much of a crush he had on me.

"But you know I'm colored."

"Italians are colored."

"Not that kind of colored," I told him.

But that didn't matter to him, and he meant it. "You are the most beautiful woman I've ever seen," he said.

He had some plan for us to marry and move to Las Vegas, and there nobody would know us, and we could live as man and wife with nobody the wiser. It was very flattering, but Joe was crazy. He was serious, but I couldn't take him seriously. I didn't like him in that way, though he was very, very, charming. I wouldn't budge an inch, and he finally lost interest, but we parted friends.

Joe sat down at the table and waved over one of the Café boys to serve us. "Give us a dozen of those beignets and a couple of coffees."

The boy quickly brought the food back, and of course Joe didn't even put out a dime. I gave the boy a nickel tip and he left happy.

Joe ate doughnut after doughnut until the powdered sugar sprinkled the blue shirt of his uniform. The man was built like a horse, tall and strong, but he ate like a pig.

"Well, you know I had to do some looking to find the dope on that Lucien fellah."

"Yes," I said, leaning forward.

Joe shrugged. "You know, it ain't that easy to get good dope on colored crime. Cops don't spend much time worrying about colored killing themselves up, but I asked around and heard some things about your sister's boyfriend."

Why was he taking so long to get it out?

"Listen, Lita. Your sister needs to watch herself, yeah. What I heard about this guy, she's knee-deep in the crapper."

"Yeah, but why? What do you know about him?"

Joe scooted his chair closer to me and whispered, "Listen. He's one sick SOB if you know what I mean."

"What?" I said, wondering if Joe was just teasing me, trying to lead me like the joker he is.

"You know I'd just tell you, but this ain't the kind of thing a man talks to a lady about."

I bolted up. "Joe, I don't have time to pussyfoot around. Do you know something?"

"Come on, calm down," he said, and gestured for me to sit. "This ain't the easy thing to say, but this guy don't just hurt women, you know, beating his girl upside the head or something. No, from what I heard he's a sicko."

Well, Mother was right. But Joe was holding more back.

"He's a suspect in a lot of colored killings. His name comes up, but like I was telling you, nobody's really spending time trying to solve those crimes. You know, colored whores ain't high up on things to do."

"My sister's no whore," I said.

Joe sighed and looked away from me. "I suppose. Running around on her husband . . . that's the kind of thing . . . you know what I'm saying? Some of my fellow policemen make use of his services. So as long as he's treating them right, they don't care what he does."

"No. You're telling me because she's playing around, that makes her a whore and nobody on the police force is going to care?"

"My buddies care. They'll make him sing soprano."

Joe laughed and bit a doughnut. "He won't be messing with married women. He won't have nothing to mess with."

I shook my head.

"And Lita, don't you even sit in the same room with this man. Don't trust him for a second—just call me."

A week before the wedding, and still not a word from Adele. Her house stayed empty and dark, and I wondered if maybe she was dead, buried in the backyard, or walled up in the back bedroom. I couldn't talk to Mother, because now her only concerns were the wedding and the bar. Anything other than that she had no time for, and that included Adele. Sick as Mother was, it was understandable. If something was going to be done for Adele, it would be up to me.

I asked for Winston's opinion, and he was frank as I ever heard him. "Listen to your mother. She knows what she's talking about. It's not your business to be sticking your nose into."

I nodded. In a few days he would be my husband, and wives should at least pretend to listen to their husbands.

I thought about calling Joe and having him go over to where Lucien lived, but I figured Adele would be there, and who knows what might happen. The cops would be ready to bust up somebody, and maybe Adele would get caught up in it. No, what I needed to do was to get Adele out of there and away from him.

The next day I cornered Daddy on the porch having a beer. "I need the car," I said.

"Girl, ain't nobody driving that car but me."

"Then you better drive me, otherwise I'm taking it."

"My, my, you don't know how to talk to your father," Daddy said, throwing his hands up like he was disgusted.

"I'm going to check on Adele, your daughter. Nobody's seen her in days."

For a moment Daddy actually looked concerned. He fished around in his pockets until he found the keys. "I saw Adele a couple days ago. With Lucien, on their way somewhere."

"How did she look? Was she okay?"

"She looked fine. Dressed to the nines like she usually do. And old Lucien was pleased with himself. Told me he was gonna take good care of my girl."

"Well, Daddy, things ain't fine. She's supposed to be in my wedding, and you know what, we haven't seen hide nor hair of her."

Daddy shrugged. "She's a big girl," he said, and his eyes darted away.

"Daddy, somebody's got to do something."

Daddy smirked. "So I'm supposed to let you use the car to go over there and drag your sister home?"

"I want to try," I said. This was as much of a conversation Daddy and I had in years. It was making me
more nervous than Lucien.

"So what you're going to do if Lucien won't let
you?"

"I don't know."

Daddy clapped his hands together, smashing a
mosquito. "Let's go," he said.

I gave Daddy directions to Lucien's, but before we even
got there, he said we were wasting our time.

"Helen took you over to that flophouse on Conti.
Lucien don't live there. That's just a place, you know,
men like to go to relax."

"You gamble there," I said.

"Yeah, that's right."

"You've played cards with Lucien?"

Again, Daddy looked away. "I've played a few
hands with him."

I wanted to grab him around the neck and bash his
head on the steering wheel.

"How come soon as anybody starts talking about
this man, they just freeze up like he's got a gun to your
head?"

Daddy laughed. "I guess you know Lucien."

We reached Conti, and Daddy pulled the car over.

"Lita, you stay your ass in the car. I'll be right back."

Now, this was one for the books: Daddy watching out for the well-being of his daughter for the very first time I could remember. I watched him walk through the trash-filled yard to the porch and knock. He seemed nervous; his walk, which always looked more like a glide, was gone. Now he plodded like he was reluctant to be there at all. But at least he was going to try to do something about Adele. I could respect him for that.

I don't know how long I sat there in that car waiting on him. Long enough to start to bake like a ham, and long enough to reconsider my opinion about how Daddy lived his life—maybe he wasn't an unredeemable pig—and long enough for me to worry about him. As I walked to the door, I slid the hairpin Mother had given me when I was old enough to date into my hand. She called it the Last Resort Pin: if they won't leave you alone, stick them someplace soft and run. It was four inches long and had a turtle-shell handle that made it easy to grip. I held the pin backward, up along my wrist, then knocked.

I heard noise: laughter, men's voices. I knocked again, then pounded the door. Finally it opened. A little dried-up man stood there, looking up at me and licking his lips. "Who you here for?" he asked, raspy whiskey voice. I could barely hear him over the noise of the party going on behind him.

"Thomas."

"Ain't no Thomas here, but you come in anyway."

"My father—he just came in about an hour ago,"

"Oh, you mean Doc."

"Doc?"

The little man shrugged. "Yeah, because he's always got something operating." He gestured for me to follow him into the next room.

Here it was in the middle of the day and it was Mardi Gras in that little shitty house. Some men sat on a busted couch that had cutoff legs, drinking from dark green bottles and yelling at each other. There was a woman there, a fat white woman who danced by herself in the middle of the room to a blues song on the radio. She hiked up her skirt, and the men roared. In the next room men sat jammed around a table; cigarette and cigar smoke hung like fog above their heads as they played cards. A pile of dollars sat dead center on the table like leaves to be burned. The half-dozen poker players eyed each other and the money and didn't seem to notice anything else—at least, Daddy didn't notice me as I watched him play out his hand. And after the man with the cockeye won the pot, Daddy didn't seem to be too much in a rush to hurry out and see about me. He just cursed the winner long and hard. He still didn't see me even when he looked up and told the fat woman to bring a whiskey. I guess he forgot what I looked like. I did see the car keys hanging out of his shirt pocket. After more cards were dealt and he focused on the new hand, I reached over and grabbed the keys and pulled them free, along with the pocket. I ripped one of

Daddy's favorite shirts, and I expected him to at least curse me, but he didn't. He just waved bye-bye like I was some goddamn child.

I drove over to Adele's. The house she had loved and fretted over was quickly falling apart, unattended in New Orleans's paint-peeling humidity. The lawn was four inches high and weed-infested. On the porch I noticed a mound of mail: weatherworn bills and a soiled letter from Rene. Oh yeah, probably letting her know what she already had to know: he was leaving her. I needed to go inside of the house. If she was dead, I wanted to see the body first. I didn't want some stranger or a neighbor or even a relative having the privilege of bearing bad news and beating us over the head with it. I walked around to the backyard, and it looked worse than the front: a rotted-out Packard rested on wood blocks, grass grew up to the running boards, and next to it was a rusted transmission. It wasn't hard to find a way in. The back door was unlocked. I knocked once, waited for a response, and knocked again. I called Adele's name as I opened the door and stepped inside. The house smelled rank. I gagged and charged outside; something was dead and reeking in there. I left the door open behind me, took off the scarf around my neck and covered my nose and mouth, and walked back in.

The smell lessened with the door open, but it still made my eyes water. Through Adele's sewing room, which she never used, and into the kitchen it was bad, real bad, and it was staggering near the oven by the door that led to Adele and Rene's bedroom. I couldn't bring myself to open that door. I ran to the front door and flung it open.

Fresh air. I could think a little more clearly. I needed to leave, find Winston or Joe, but I couldn't. This was up to me. This was my sister. Everybody seemed to think she had it coming; whatever Lucien did or would do to her, she deserved it.

I calmed myself and prepared to check the bedroom, where I was sure the smell came from. I remembered the hairpin. I slid it from my hair and headed for the bedroom.

I shoved the door open. Nothing unusual: even the bed was made, but some things were missing. A lamp, a small desk she wrote letters at. I finally pinpointed it; the closet. The smell had to be coming from there. The door was locked. I twisted at the handle a number of times, but it held. I reached for the letter opener in my purse and gave it a shot. The lock gave right away. I shoved the door open and jumped backward. Nothing, no one sprang out to get me. I came forward and tried to make out what was inside. The floor! Something was lying there. I waited for my eyes to adjust. A shape, a mound, lay on the floor. I reached in and felt hair. . . . I fell backward in a panic until I realized I was clutching

Adele's mink. She loved that coat Rene had worked so hard to give her. She barely could wait for the weather to cool to flaunt it. If she ran off, the coat would have gone with her. When I was sure she wasn't dead somewhere in the bedroom, I relaxed enough to notice just how bad that smell was once again. Something was dead, even if it wasn't in the bedroom. I returned to the kitchen and realized the smell was coming from there. Then I kicked something, glanced down, and saw the ragged ball of fur near the oven—that fat cat of Adele's she was so crazy about.

75

I arrived home to see Winston sitting on the steps of the porch, head hanging down, like a tired old man.

He looked up, surprised to see me driving Daddy's car.

"Hi, Winston," I said. His face looked as strained as a flag blowing in a strong wind.

"Where have you been?"

I looked away. I didn't want to lie to him, but neither did I want to tell him the truth.

"Did you find her?"

"Find who?"

"Adele."

"No, I didn't."

"Your Daddy just walked up and explained how you stole his car."

"Yeah, I guess I did."

"I don't know why you're spending so much time worrying about your sister. It's not your business. If we were already married, I wouldn't allow you to do what you're doing. You've got to mind your own business."

"Listen, Winston, she's my sister. It's my responsibility. It's got nothing to do with you."

Winston shook his head and pointed to his ears. "You got to listen to me. A woman shouldn't be running around doing something dangerous. I'm trying to set you straight."

I let him have his say. Then I caught his eye. "I want to call off the wedding."

"What?" he said, standing up at attention.

"You heard me."

"The wedding's Sunday."

"Right now, I couldn't care any less," I said.

"But—we made plans—"

He reached for me, but I walked right by him into the house and slammed the door in his face.

Three days later, I allowed Winston to come over to the house. It seemed pretty damn silly—we were to be married in two days, and I didn't know if I wanted to see him, at least not yet anyway—but today was the wedding rehearsal. If I told him to get lost now, the wedding would be off for good. We took a long walk through the neighborhood, arm in arm. I even put my head on his shoulder, and that did it. All was right for him; he knew he was forgiven.

"Hey, you know, I'm sorry I bit your head off," he said. "I was worried about you, that's all."

"That's okay. I'm not mad anymore."

"You ready to get married?" he asked, barely hiding his nervousness.

"You bet I am," I said, and kissed him.

At the house the whole family was excited. Mother was out of bed and getting everything ready for the rehearsal. Even Daddy was home, helping Ava and Ana practice marching through the house.

"Where have you two been?" Mother asked.

"Walking," I said, and snuggled against Winston.

I think Mother blushed before she turned away and called to Daddy to load the girls in the car. We were going to church.

Because Adele wasn't there to be my bridesmaid, I decided not to have one. Mother couldn't stop trying to soften me up like I was a leathery pot roast in a pressure cooker. She had so many suggestions—Cousin Rita, Cousin Lucy, and so on—but she finally figured out I wouldn't change my mind. This was my wedding, and Mother had to understand that. Turning up the burner wouldn't change anything.

Adele is my sister. She might have done wrong and acted stupidly, but blood meant something to us Du Champs—or at least, I thought it did.

78

Mother woke me out of a deep sleep like she would do when she had a bone to pick with me, but there was no anger in her eyes. She sat at the edge of my bed, huffing, almost unable to catch her breath.

"Lita," she said, and wiped her face with the hem of her apron. "You think I'm being heartless, but it's not that simple. I'm going to tell you because the worst has already happened to Adele, and you need to be prepared for it."

Mother had to stop, too winded to keep going. I watched as she struggled for air. Then after a moment where I thought she'd pass out, she caught herself and began as though she was resuming a story she had begun some time ago. She told it in a harsh whisper, as though someone or something might hear besides me in the sleeping house. "Adele, my precious spoiled little one, always wanted so much. Rene knew she played around, but what could he expect with a beautiful young woman, alone for months at a time in a city like New Orleans? But no one expected Lucien to walk into the picture. I knew there was a sadness to her, but I didn't know she wanted to die. Soon as she took up with Lucien it was just a matter of time for the other shoe to drop. Vain as she was, she didn't suspect Lucien's interest had to do with more than just easy cheating. This mess started long before she had set eyes on Lucien. Adele just didn't know she was just a prop in his little revenge play. Her birth mother got this started long ago."

"Adele's not my sister?"

"Shut up and listen," Mother said, flatly.

"But I—"

"Just listen," she said, again.

When I first heard Lucien's name twenty years ago in 1926, it was whispered that he had killed a girl, but killings happened like rain in the Ninth Ward. You could always blame a shooting on the heat and humidity or whiskey. But what people were saying about this Lucien was different. Just a baby, barely fourteen, from what people said, this well-built and well-spoken boy had beaten a girl to death. Back then, news in the colored wards spread like Indian fire. Seems like everybody had something to say about the boy in a man's body, the killer with such a handsome face. When I first heard about this child, I wasn't yet married, but I had finished school and was running the family fish market, and from where my stall was, on the edge of the Vieux Carré, I saw and heard much of what went on in New Orleans. An old woman who picked over my fish and complained so much I refused to sell to her pointed out Lucien: "See, there he go, just a overgrown boy, but you know he done killed a girl and going round bragging about it."

We expected someone in the girl's family would handle it—track the boy down and make him pay. The funny thing was that Lucien became not just a man but a big man because of killing that girl. From the way some imbeciles sounded, they admired him for bashing the girl's head in. I knew this girl. She was poor and ugly and black as tar. So poor she dragged the streets begging from women and trying to whore herself to men. So poor nobody missed her when she disappeared. But Lucien bragged about it, went around describing what he had done. And nobody did a damned thing about it. He found the right person to kill. Yes, he was a big man, even though he was barely fourteen. We'd see him in church in his short pants, and people would say, "There goes that boy! Got the gall to come to church with that sin on his soul," but nobody stopped him at the door and threw him out.

A few years later no one mentioned that girl when they talked about him. If anything, they had praise for how the young man dressed and how much money he had in his pocket. Now he had girls working for him just like the girl he killed—poor, young, and stupid. Lucien bought them clothes, fed them, and put them out to work. You couldn't miss Lucien's girls, walking Canal no matter how late and what kind of weather. They didn't wait for a man to come to them. I saw one grab hold of a sailor, and no matter what the sailor did, she wouldn't let go, even after he knocked her down. Finally he tossed a few coins on the ground to get her out of his hair. Those girls worked till they looked like half-dead plow horses. Lucien knew how to get the best out of them, the last nickel from their bedraggled bodies. If they wanted to see another day, they better bring Lucien his due. He worked those girls into the ground until only the most desperate man would want what they had to offer. Then Lucien's whores disappeared; the half-dozen dark-skinned girls no longer worked the streets around the fish market. I thought he'd headed elsewhere with the girls, maybe because he fell behind to Barnes, the cop who worked that part of the Quarter. Barnes was the type of cop who wanted his money in advance of whenever he said he needed it. Maybe Lucien's whores couldn't cover Barnes's fee, and he headed for a cheaper neighborhood to work.

I was wrong. Lucien returned, but the girls were no longer black and thin and with short rough hair. No, while they weren't exactly café au lait, they were close, with good, long hair. He didn't have as many of them, just three, but he was proud of the replacements, strutting through the markets while the girls went about the business of being seen. They were better-looking and fairer and they didn't work nearly as hard as the previous girls to please Lucien because I'm sure they made far more money. Colored men would stretch till it hurt to pay for their affections, and white men found a bargain, girls who were much better-looking than almost all the white whores, and for less money.

Lucien was on top of the world. He dressed even better than he had before, happily ruining fine suits wearing them on the hottest or wettest days, and he bought an automobile before most colored people had one, let alone such a young man barely out of his teens, and now that he had success, he even began carrying himself with more maturity. He rarely chased girls down busy streets, dragging them by the hair into an alley for a stiff whipping. If he had to administer a beating, he did it in private. Unfortunately, the alley behind my stall is what he considered private.

One of the new girls was the one I saw Lucien beat into a heap because she didn't heel like he wanted her to heel. She refused to go with a few too many johns, and one or two she cut with that knife she kept in her sleeve. Lucien beat her viciously on each of those occasions, and afterward she had to attract customers with a swollen face and blackened eyes or she could expect more trouble from Lucien. After each beating she worked almost as hard as the dark-skinned girls, but sooner or later she returned to the obstinate ways that enraged him.

Her name was Ruby and she was from St. Charles. Something about seeing this pretty young girl made me want to help her even if I'd end up having to deal with Lucien. It was her pride. Lucien could bust her and try to break her, but she refused to give in. One early Friday morning, must have been around four in the morning, on my way to the stall, after going to the docks to get first shot at the catch, I saw Lucien and his three girls at the Café du Monde having coffee and beignets. Two of the girls sat almost on top of Lucien, acting like giddy school-children out with their father, but Ruby sat away from them, staring out at the Mississippi, not even paying Lucien the least amount of attention. I stopped and watched them from a safe distance. Lucien was too busy playing at being the generous, attentive daddy to notice me. But Ruby turned her head away from the busy river and looked in my direction, and even with the cover of darkness she knew I was staring at her, wondering how she'd fallen so far. I hurried on because her interest piqued Lucien's interest, and soon they were all watching me walk to my stall.

I couldn't stop thinking about her. She didn't act like any of the spiritless, broken prostitutes I'd seen working the Vieux Carré.

I called her over when Lucien was out of earshot

and offered her a sandwich. She wiped her nose on a soiled sleeve and rolled her eyes, and she took the food with such disdain I wanted to snatch the sandwich and tell her to go to hell.

"Who you think you are? Some kinda saint? Yeah?"

I couldn't help but feel good about doing what I was doing even if she did point out something I couldn't deny, but she came for the lunches I made for her.

She depended on them and needed them. Her visits weren't very long, just the amount of time it took for her to wolf down the man-size po' boy and to wipe her mouth and eye me like a wary dog not wanting to be messed with. She stood off to the side of the stall so as not to catch Lucien's eye. I was grateful for that, getting seen as much as I was with her; the tightness of her dress and the snugness of the blouse and how she wore her hair down was already causing people to talk.

"See, I thought you was one of them do-good sisters," Ruby said. "Had my fill of them. Say all they gon' do for you, then what they end up doing is lockin' you up making you pray like it gon' change something."

I didn't have much to say in these conversations, because she wasn't interested. She'd just turn her head or walk away if I did more than nod. I soon realized that was what she wanted to do—ignore everything and anybody she could get away with ignoring.

"I don't think about nothing—just let them do that business unless I'm hungry. Then I think about chicken or biscuits or whatever I have a taste for."

Made sense to me. If I had to put up with some fat, sweating, stinking pig of a man inside of me, I wouldn't want to think either.

The problem for her was, she tried to treat Lucien the same way, but he taught her the lesson over and over again: it can't be done. She couldn't ignore him without lots of pain, but she tried to over and over again, with the same result: another beating.

I realized after hearing Ruby go on about other things—how even though she had beautiful brown skin she was white, and how she was going to have a stall like mine once she had enough saved, and how one day she and Lucien would get married, and have a family—she wasn't right in the head. It took a while to see it, but it made sense. She didn't answer questions because she was smart enough to know she wasn't smart enough. Her pride and anger came out of that—of not wanting to let anyone think they had something on her.

Lucien knew how to pick them. Probably stole her right off the front porch. "Come here, I want you to be my wife," is all he had to say, and I'm sure she left a grieving mother behind to have an adventure with the handsome man.

Sometime later Ruby came to my stall for a sandwich, looking more radiant than I had ever seen her, like an Egyptian princess, her hair beautifully full and dark with curls and her brown skin shining like it was oiled gold. My heart sank because I could tell before she said a word, she was pregnant.

While she ate, knowing she'd probably ignore me, I asked her, "Ruby, are you pregnant?"

She turned to look at me and while chewing she answered, "Don't it show?"

"Well, yes."

"It don't bother me. Men come beggin' now, wanting mother's milk."

"But you got to stop. Go home. You're a pregnant woman."

"Yeah, but Lucien say I got to keep working."

That was that. She wouldn't say another word about it. A blond man with a beard so thick it made him look like a billy goat almost knocked an old lady over trying to get to Ruby. She went off with him, still chewing that sandwich like she didn't have a care.

Soon as I sold out of fish, I went looking for Lucien. I found him at the café sipping coffee, reading the paper like some kind of gentleman.

"Excuse me," I said, and he looked at me with a warm smile.

He hid his youth well, so tall and well built it was hard to believe he was still a teen.

"Good afternoon," he said, and pulled a seat out for me.

"Helen Du Champ," I said, extending my hand.

"Lucien Fauré," he said, and kissed my hand. I wiped it on the bottom of the chair.

"I want to talk to you about Ruby."

"Ruby? Yeah, you're the one who feeds her sandwiches. Very generous of you."

"She's pregnant."

"Yes, it's a miracle," he said with a cruel smile.

"What are you going to do? She can't keep working."

"It is one of the hazards of the job."

"She's carrying a child. If it were your child, you wouldn't be so cold.

Lucien laughed. "But it's not. It's nice you're concerned for Ruby, but don't you worry. I take care of my girls."

I wanted to grab that heavy marble table and flip it over on top of him. I wanted to bash his beautiful teeth in, but I stood there seething. "Where did you find her?" I heard myself asking.

He laughed. "I never seen a colored woman or even a Creole get so red."

"Where did you find her!" I asked as my voice rose to almost a scream.

His pleasant demeanor evaporated.

"Don't make a scene," he said, in a voice so commanding that it made me want to listen to him, like Ruby and his girls did.

I opened my mouth to shout again. Lucien

sprang up to grab me, but I slipped away from him.

"Listen," he said, now composed again. He sat down and gestured for me to sit, but I refused.

"There's no reason for bad feelings. I intend to do right by Ruby. In fact I'm sending her back to St. Charles soon as I can afford to buy a train ticket." He smiled that smile, and I wanted to believe him. That smile was like slipping into a hot bath with your wrists cut.

"Sure," I said. "That sounds swell."

I wouldn't allow myself to glance back at him as I left the café. That man could turn the Virgin Mary into a whore.

Ruby stopped coming for sandwiches. She wouldn't look in my direction when she walked by with a john, but she couldn't hide the shiner on her left eye.

Lucien solved the problem—beat the hell out of her, and that was that.

When my father came by for Sunday dinner, I spoke to him about Ruby. He was old now and not always alert, but he still had a sharp mind for business. How else could he afford two families and various illegitimate children around town?

Father was an Irishman who had come over in 1869 with, as he liked to tell us, enough stolen jewels so he never had to work. Instead he bought and sold jewels and made enough to cover his losses at the card table and his obligations. Mother he treated as a second wife and not as a octoroon mistress, which is to say he only beat her every now and then. Unlike those Irish bastards who took colored lovers, for the most part he treated us well. I knew he was my father even if he did live on the other side of town, with blond children and a red-haired wife. Certainly he took care of his children. After Mother died he signed over to me the house I had been raised in. He also set up the fish business, talking to all the right Irishmen so I could *passe blanche* into the French Quarter world set off for white businessmen. He tried to do for Dot, but she wasn't interested in school or working. The only reason she was excited about Father buying her that sewing machine was that she could make herself look as good as blond southern belles who could afford European dresses. Even now, though she was the best seamstress you'd ever meet, she spent so much time beating people out of their money, she constantly had to find new customers to fleece.

Father would come by after mass at that Catholic church across town where colored people weren't wanted. I made the same dinner for him every week, corned beef and cabbage with boiled potato and a dessert of bread pudding.

"Helen," he said, "I don't know why you're concerned about this woman. Go give some money to the Sisters of Mercy, if that'll make you feel better."

"It's this man, this Lucien, he's a mad dog, beating pregnant women and worse. It's not right."

Father shook his head. "So what would you have me do?"

I didn't say anything. Father's mouth narrowed, and his ruddy face flushed redder. "Do you want him gone?"

"Yes, I want him gone."

"You know what you're asking?"

I nodded.

"I can do this for you, but I hope you know what this colored man can expect."

"He's a child killer. Whatever happens to him, he deserves it."

"Barnes will take care of it. Yes, it's what the man likes to do."

"Barnes is on Lucien's payroll."

"Barnes is on everyone's payroll, but he likes beating niggers. Yes, he does." Father laughed, and I poured him a whiskey and watched him smoke his cigar.

The next few days went as usual around the Vieux Carré. I'd see Lucien sauntering somewhere, and he'd wave to me like we were the best of friends. Ruby's black eye had cleared up, and she stopped at my stall for a quick chat.

"You got anything to eat?"

I handed her my lunch: bread, cheese, and an apple.

"Where's the po' boy? This don't make a person want to eat in all this heat."

But she ate it hastily. She finished and looked around for something more, but all I had was raw fish.

"I got to eat," she said, and hurried away in search of food. She was eating for two, and Lucien wasn't feeding her enough for one.

The next day, late in the afternoon, Barnes moved to clean up the Vieux Carré from ruffians and undesirables.

I didn't see it start, but someone told me they saw Lucien at his table in the Café du Monde. Barnes and two other barrel-chested cops walked over to Lucien, and without a word, Barnes cracked him upside the head with a blackjack. With my own eyes I saw Lucien fling the three cops away and run for his life. Legs churning in the humid air, he had made it past my stall and almost to Canal Street when the police, blowing hard, caught up with him and commenced to kick and punch him. I thought Barnes would have killed him right there, but Lucien's girls came running, screaming like banshees.

"Get off him, you crackers!" The girl with the gap-teeth leaped onto the back of Barnes, scratching at his eyes, riding him like a horse. Barnes peeled Gap-Tooth off and pounded her with both fists until she cowered helplessly. The other girl, sobbing and pulling hair from her head, stood there watching

Lucien get more of the same. Then I noticed Ruby and her big pregnant belly, Lucien's gun in her hand. If she'd pointed it, if they'd noticed it, they'd have killed her right there in the street. I ran from behind my stall, wrapped my arms around her, led her to my stall, and forced her down to the ground. So stunned to see Lucien brought down, she was as pliant as a pole-axed calf. I took the gun from her hand and stuffed it into my purse.

The cops gathered up Lucien and hurled him into a paddy wagon. They tossed him in and then the gap-toothed girl. The other girl hopped up into the wagon like she didn't want to be left behind. Suddenly Ruby came out of her stupor and pushed me away and shouted for the police to wait. "Where you taking him? I oughta go. That's my husband! I'm going too!"

Barnes looked at her and saw that swollen stomach. He shook his head as if he wanted nothing to do with her.

I tried to pull her aside. "Get out of my way!" she said, scratching at my face, pulling my hair. She did everything to break away, but I held on.

Laughing, Barnes watched Ruby beat me.

"You got your hands filled with that little lady. You want me to take her off of your hands?"

"No!" I said. "I can handle her." I pinned her arms, and she watched helplessly as the paddy wagon drove off.

"Leave me alone!" Ruby said, shouting into my face.

"Come on, Ruby. It's over. Did you want to go to jail? To some women's prison to have your baby?"

"I don't care!"

"No, you do care."

Ruby stopped fighting, and I unwrapped my arms from around her. She sagged to the cobblestones, crying.

I took her home to the empty house on Gravier Street.

"This big house is yours?" she asked as I led her inside.

I nodded.

"Just you?"

"My mother died not too long ago. My sister used to live here, but she's out on her own. Aunt Odie is supposed to come stay with me, but she's not here just yet."

Adele looked around the sparely furnished parlor where Mother had been waked not a year ago.

"Don't you get scared living here by yourself? You must see ghosts and all that."

"No, not at this house."

"How you know? Do you be looking for them?"

"Yes, I looked for them, but I didn't see anything for you to be worried about."

Ruby was about ready to bolt as though she had never lived under a roof in her entire life. Where did

Lucien have them staying, on a hammock slung between two trees?

"Ruby, you're welcome to live here till you have your baby."

She rolled her eyes in disgust. "I don't want no baby. I want Lucien."

"There isn't a thing you can do now except for having the baby."

Ruby put her hands on her hips and glared at me. "Why'd you make them policemen take Lucien away? You know you did!"

"I didn't have nothing to do with that."

Ruby smirked. "You a do-gooder. That's what do-gooders do. Mess in other people's business."

"I don't have anything good to say for Lucien. That man is a snake, and all you got to do is open your eyes. He just wants to use women and hurt them and worse."

"What you know about him? He's good to me."

"That's what you call good? Oh, Lord. Lucien saw you coming."

Ruby turned her pregnant body around and wobbled for the front door.

"You don't have no place else to go!" I said.

She opened the door and stood there, framed in the doorway by the darkness outside. Finally she shut the door and turned to me, looking sheepish. "Why do you want me here?" she asked.

I sighed. She was trying her best to figure out

what I was up to. But that was understandable; any drop of kindness that Lucien offered was sure to be followed up by a bucketful of misery.

"So you and the baby you're carrying can have a chance."

"Why do you care? You want this baby? You want my baby?" She laughed at me long and hard. I stood there unable to say a word, watching her pat her belly. "I'll tell you what, I'll let you have the baby. What I'm gonna do with it, anyway?"

"I didn't say I wanted the baby. I said I don't want you on the streets, expecting a baby."

Ruby ignored me and started poking around the house like an alley cat spying out all the trouble it could get into. Then she saw the half room off of the front door. "You sleep in there?"

"No, that's just a nook. My bed can't fit."

I opened the door for her so she could see how bare, unfurnished, and small it was.

She looked the room over with the same interest she'd given the po' boys I gave her.

"You saying I can stay here?" She was giggling to herself even though that four-by-seven box was cramped and dusty and smelled faintly of rotting wood. "Suits me fine."

"Are you sure? There's a bigger, nicer room at the back of the house."

"I like this one. It's just the right size."

Later, I found out the appeal of the room wasn't

its size but its location. She wanted a quick exit if she needed it.

Maybe Ruby had forgotten or had never known what it meant to be indolent, but she practiced it faithfully now, as if she were making up for all those long, hot days working for Lucien. At first I worried about leaving her alone, fearing she'd grab a handful of silverware and disappear, but instead of larceny she engaged in sloth, lazing away in the love seat near the front window, watching people, listening to the radio, eating peanuts I'd bring from the market. Each day she ate more and more, until now she was working on a ten-pound sack.

I'd return home from the fish market and she'd be rooted in place like some housebound banana tree, getting bigger of belly with each passing day.

Father came by for his usual Sunday dinner and saw her in the same love seat he used to share with Mother. Ruby ignored Father, not even bothering to look up from the crocheting she pretended to be doing.

Father glared at her, then turned to me. "That's the woman you say needs so much of your help? Jay-us, she looks healthful enough."

Father said this loud enough so Ruby had to hear, but now that she was content, she didn't bother with insults. Yawning, she leaned over and reached into the ten-pound bag of peanuts and grabbed another handful.

"After she breaks water, what are you going to do? How long you going to support her?"

I shrugged, not having an idea.

"Better think 'bout it. Else you could be doing this forever."

Aunt Odie arrived. And her arrival scared Ruby more than Lucien ever had. She appeared midmorning in the window Ruby had spent the last few weeks staring out of, popping up before her like a ghoul from Saint Louis Cemetery, frightening her so, she fell head over heels backward and, big as she was, went running through the house with me chasing her, shouting, "It's Aunt Odie! It's Aunt Odie come to visit." Soon enough she calmed down, but I did have to mop up the trail of water she left. Afterward Ruby finally decided to move her body from off of the couch into that closet she said she wanted to sleep in but never did. Aunt Odie did that to people.

I long ago had gotten use to that death-mask face, but for the rest of the world, including Father and whoever else, they could no more expect to see the face of God than a smile from Aunt Odie's harsh face. She was taller than most men, dark-skinned, with a elongated face and high cheekbones and a flat forehead. Her deep-set dark eyes and oversize jaw gave people the impression she was a walking death's-head. She was much younger than Mother, and even though they were distant cousins and not sisters, they were very close. Aunt Odie wasn't able to go to school like Mother, but she was very well read. As a child she had the same face, and children were too cruel to be trusted, books were her companions, and so Aunt Odie talked unlike anyone I knew, educated as she was ugly. She knew the world like the back of her hand, though she never traveled. She spoke foreign languages and knew the Bible better than ministers. Now, Aunt Odie worked for a very rich white woman who was half blind and did not care about how disturbing Aunt Odie's face was. She did value her skills as a nurse. Aunt Odie spent as much of her free time with Mother as possible, and when Mother died, she still came to look after me even after I was running things well enough on my own. I looked forward to her visits, and she always brought me presents, books or writing paper. I had mentioned Ruby to her in passing, and her reaction was not her usual nod, but one of those blood-freezing stares.

"Don't bring shame to yourself. She doesn't deserve your worry and pity. If you give it, you will live to regret it."

I didn't argue with Aunt Odie—there was rarely any reason to—so she was surprised when I said, "But . . ."

"But what? It's hard enough to be colored without taking on the miseries of those that have chosen misfortune."

Then I explained the situation to Aunt Odie. The

whole sad story of Lucien and Ruby and what my father had done to stop him. Aunt Odie shook her head as though she couldn't understand anything I had been saying. I began to repeat myself, but she held her hand up to stop me. "I heard every word you said. I am not deaf, but I am surprised your father allowed you to involve yourself in this."

She turned as I put down her satchel. "Tomorrow I will talk to this girl and find out exactly what this business is all about."

"You really don't have to worry yourself. Nothing is going to get out of hand."

"Your mother would not have forgiven me if I didn't see about you and how you were conducting yourself. I will have a talk with this Miss Ruby first thing tomorrow morning."

She shut the door, and for the next hour I could hear her deep voice reciting the rosary with a vengeance.

Usually I am up at least an hour before sunrise, and I'm almost always the first one to stir, but this morning Aunt Odie had beaten me and was already making breakfast. But more unusual than that was the sight of Ruby awake before noon. I was used to seeing her twisted up on that love seat with a sheet drawn over her head like some corpse killed in the midst of a embrace.

Ruby sat at the table with a plate of eggs and

ham before her. Her head was downcast as though she was praying.

"Join us," Aunt Odie said.

I did, across from Ruby. I wanted to see her face. Oh, my Lord! She looked so much like a child. Somehow Aunt Odie had scrubbed her clean of bitterness and contempt with plain old fear. "Ruby and I had a talk last night."

I nodded.

"We understand each other."

I nodded again.

"She's agreed to a cleansing ceremony."

"A cleansing ceremony?"

Aunt Odie sat down with her breakfast and looked the way she did when she had something she needed to take the time to explain to me. "I know your mother didn't approve of you knowing anything about the spirit world," she said. "I wouldn't do anything to go against her wishes, but as an adult you need to make your owns decisions."

"Decisions? Are you taking her to see Father Marks?"

Aunt Odie rolled her eyes. "Of course not. What has that man ever done for anybody? He's a imbecile, and I know for a fact he has nothing good to say about colored people."

"Are you talking about voodoo?" I blurted, figuring Aunt Odie would laugh at me. Her black eyes just fixed on me like she intended to crack me upside the head.

"Did I say something wrong?" I asked.

"Didn't your mother show you any of her books?"

"She showed me books, but I don't know what kind of books you're talking about."

"Did she mention the Countess?"

"Who?"

"Zabeau Countess."

Ruby finally glanced up from her breakfast, looking as radiant and healthy as a horse. "You ain't heard of her? Even I've heard of that woman, and everybody know I don't know nothing," she said, like a breathless child.

Aunt Odie patted her hand to hush her. "Zabeau Countess is a spiritual healer. She's not like these charlatans you see around this city offering advice and wisdom from the afterlife or from spirits from the old country. They offer fool's gold, when Zabeau Countess has true power and insight."

Aunt Odie had never talked this way before. I thought she was Catholic like everybody else, but she was a damn voodooist.

"What's going to happen? What are they going to do to her?"

Ruby suddenly sat erect, waiting to hear what she would be going through.

"It's a baptism," Aunt Odie said flatly.

"A baptism? Isn't she baptized?"

"Oh, no. I'm not baptized. I know that for a fact."

Aunt Odie glanced at Ruby and silenced her without a word.

I picked at my eggs and grits, but I had no appetite. Aunt Odie had come along and made a complicated situation even more so.

"This baptism is a exorcism. Zabeau Countess will help to change Ruby's future and the poisoned future of her baby."

I shook my head. This scared me to death, hearing Aunt Odie talking about voodoo like Easter Mass.

"You are welcome to come with us to see Zabeau Countess. Since you have been acting as Ruby's protector, your presence would be beneficial. Zabeau Countess will plan the ceremony and tell Ruby what to expect and what she needs to do to purify her soul."

I didn't know what to say. I didn't want to go.

"I have my fish shop."

"When you're finished. We'll come for you."

"Good," I said. But I didn't mean that. I wanted nothing to do with voodoo or this Zabeau Countess.

I sold the last of the shrimp and packed the rest of the fish and remaining ice for dinner. It wasn't much after noon. Usually my last customer wouldn't be for a few more hours, but I sold cheap to leave early. Now at least I had a reason to miss Ruby and Aunt Odie. They couldn't expect me to wait in the hot sun for them. Before I reached Canal Street I saw a tall, rail-thin black woman dressed all in white, escorting a very pregnant woman who was also head to toe in white, and from a distance appeared to be white. But as they approached I couldn't pretend it wasn't Aunt Odie and Ruby. They tracked me down like two-legged bloodhounds.

"Hello, you two. Going to see that Countess woman?" I said. I stopped fast to speak to them, because they were so purposeful in their walking that I thought they'd leave me be so I could go home and wash the fish from my hands and hair and sleep before they returned with stories about some witch and the miracles she worked.

"What are you stopping for? Come," Aunt Odie said, without breaking stride, and I had no choice but to follow. Lord knows I tried to avoid this, but the train had already left the station.

"Where are we going?" I asked as I fell in behind them.

"Where we need to go," Aunt Odie said.

We walked so long that Ruby had to sit and find her wind. Then we caught the ferry downriver below the city to where moss-covered cypress trees were so plentiful I had to look twice to see the shore. We disembarked at a clearing and followed the passengers, most of whom were colored; but there was a finely dressed white couple who looked like they had no business at that part of the river.

"Come on," Aunt Odie said.

We walked around a bend, and there was the town in front of us. It was so small and countrified it could have been a boil on New Orleans' backside.

"You call this a town?"

"I call it a town," Aunt Odie said, gravely, "because people here call it a town."

She had to be joking. About the only thing to see in this town was two colored kids playing in the dirt.

We walked on a road so rutted it made more sense to walk alongside instead of on it. Poor Ruby couldn't go much farther. Spying a shady patch of grass, she sat down so quickly she rolled backward, her legs flipping into the air.

"Just up there and we're done," Aunt Odie said. She pointed to a house that even from a distance I could see was near collapse. But it was a big house, like a plantation mansion. "I'll go ahead. Come along when she's ready," she said, and hurried on.

I glanced at Ruby. The load she carried was getting bigger each day. Soon she'd be ready to birth. Walks to the edge of nowhere made no sense for a woman in her state.

"Caught your breath, no?"

Ruby looked shaky.

"Don't rush. We got all the time in the world."

But Ruby surprised me and began a slow, unsteady amble. I hoped she would have changed her mind, give up on the idea that a witch could work magic and miracles. I took her arm and helped her make those last dozen yards.

"Ruby, do you want to go through with this?" I asked as we stepped onto the dangerously sagging porch of the house of Zabeau Countess.

Ruby didn't notice or didn't care about the state of ruin.

"What do you think she's going to do for you?" I asked.

Ruby looked at me. "I want her to help me get Lucien back. I want her to make him be nice to me."

Lord, whatever dubious miracles this Zabeau Countess worked, changing Lucien wasn't something even Jesus could do.

I knocked softly at the door, probably the only solid, unrotten wood in the whole house, hoping maybe they wouldn't hear me and I could hightail it back to the ferry.

Ruby wasn't having it. She nudged me aside with that big pregnant belly and beat on the door until it opened.

I thought this Zabeau Countess would look like some witch doctor with a bone in her nose. The woman who stood there scrutinizing us looked more like a nun than nuns do. She was all in white like Aunt Odie, but she wore a kerchief on her head and she was barefoot. Her hair had gone straight gray, but her skin seemed unusually smooth. The placid expression on her face unnerved me, even as she continued to look us over.

"Welcome," she said in a whisper of a voice, and stood aside for us to enter.

Inside, the house smelled of mold and wood rot and the sweet incense they use at mass, and it was as dark as if all the windows were covered or boarded. Candles burned on the mantelpiece above the fireplace and at the dining table where Aunt Odie was sitting, sharing the table with the white couple we had seen earlier. Zabeau Countess turned her attention to Ruby. "So this is the troubled one. What is your name, sister?"

"Ruby." She looked down at the ground she couldn't see because of the size of her stomach.

"You have been sullied in this life."

Ruby didn't say anything.

"But you still love the man who violated you."

"I want him back."

"But if having him back means suffering even more than you already have, you still want him?"

"Yes," Ruby said.

Zabeau Countess smiled.

"You are willing to give your life for this man. You would do anything for him?"

"I want him to love me."

Zabeau Countess sighed and took Ruby's hand. "Yours is a graveyard love. You are poisoned and need to be cleansed. Sister Odie was right."

"You can get him back for me?" Ruby asked.

"What would getting him back do? As long as you want him, you will never be loved."

"I don't want to be loved," Ruby said. "I want him."

"After the ceremony, if you still desire him, you can have him. But I doubt that you will."

"How are you going to do that?" Ruby asked, but Zabeau Countess gestured for her to be quiet. Then she took her by the hand and led her to the table.

Then I heard that woman's whispery voice like moth wings, chiding me. "Unbeliever, you come too. Don't be frightened of what you don't know. Come to the table."

With all their burning eyes upon me, making me feel naked and on fire with embarrassment, I came to them, sitting as far from the edge of the table as I could. From where Zabeau Countess sat, the candles encircled her head like a burning halo, and behind her was the altar, made of candles and toys and brightly colored ribbons.

"Sister Helen, do be aware that what we do isn't of the devil or unchristian. We believe in life and in God and the saints. Simply, we have more saints than the church recognizes. We also worship them differently. Don't believe everything that you hear about voodooists." Finally, she looked away from me and turned her attention to Ruby. "Tonight, you and our guests will join in with the other believers and dance

and sing along the river. Then we'll share communion. And then you will be ready," Zabeau Countess
said.

"Ready for what? Ruby asked.

"Ready to ask the saints for what you desire."
Aunt Odie stepped over and stood behind Ruby and
put her hands on her shoulders. "You should all know
I'm the one who brought Sister Ruby to the ceremony. My niece told me about Ruby's sad life, and I
just did not think she would be worthy to join Sister
Zabeau, but after talking to her I knew she was ready
for the ceremony."

Aunt Odie began swaying and turning about;
dancing. This was something I've never seen her do
and thought she disapproved of. Zabeau Countess
threw her head back and shouted something that got
the white couple stirring, dancing as wildly as Aunt
Odie.

This went long enough for me to want to laugh,
but I knew if I gave in a little I wouldn't be able to
stop.

Zabeau Countess noticed I hadn't joined them
and looked at me like she had looked at Ruby earlier.
"Why do you hold back?"

I shook my head. Zabeau Countess snorted.
"How will you dance at your own ceremony?"

"My ceremony? This isn't for me. It's for Ruby."

"Didn't Sister Odie explain to you about this
gathering?"

"No, but this has nothing to do with me."

"Yes, girl. I saw you in my dream, and the path you walk is the same path as Sister Ruby."

Now I was mad. I've done some things in my life I regretted, but I wasn't standing for the insult of being compared to Ruby.

"What're you saying! I haven't done none of what Ruby's done."

"Sister, we're all sinners."

"I sin, but my sins are nothing like her sins."

Zabeau Countess stared at me with unblinking eyes.

"I should be going."

"Sister, you need saving."

"Saving from what? I go to mass. I go to confession. I take communion."

Zabeau Countess sighed, took my hand, and pulled me close, whispering into my ear. "Your fate is entwined with Ruby's. You have taken responsibility for her, and you will share in her misery. . . ."

She talked on about cleansing and the importance of joining the ceremony, but I let it go in one ear and out the other. I was determined to leave, but I didn't want to make a scene; I didn't want to embarrass Aunt Odie if I could help it. Another knock at the door, and Zabeau Countess moved so slowly to answer, the knocks became so urgent, I almost pushed her aside and yanked it open myself. One more white couple head to toe in white sauntered in

and were escorted to the table. But before introduc-
tions were made, the front door opened again, and
there stood a fierce-looking, powerfully built colored
man. He wore what had to be a turban and a white
smock with leggings, and he carried a long, narrow
drum decorated with seashells along the sides.

"Zabeau Countess! The sun sets!" he shouted,
pounding the drum, and returned outside. You'd
think he was a black Pied Piper, the way everyone
followed him, clapping and dancing, until they
reached the river. Torches were arranged along the
water's edge like some flaming wall. Others had come
and were setting down platters of roasted meat and
bowls of fruit. That drum, joined by more drums,
reverberated in my skull like cannon fire. I needed to
flee, try to find my way back to the landing, even
though it was dark now and I hardly knew what
direction to go. More drummers joined the cacoph-
ony, jarring the earth, sending the half-crazed
dancers into fits and swoons. I couldn't bring myself
to look at Aunt Odie and Ruby's conniption fits, but
no one else found the sight of a pregnant woman
jumping about like a lunatic bothersome. Zabeau
Countess helped Ruby out of her white robe and led
her stark naked to the river.

The white couple stripped too, and soon everyone had, all of them naked to the world, running to
the water. Even Aunt Odie, stiff and grim, stripped
and danced to the river and waded in. Only Zabeau

Countess seemed to have her wits about her, but then she began to shout, and they all froze to listen to her.

"Spirits of the Loa, hear our prayers! Send us your cleansing fire!"

One of the drummers yanked a torch from the ground and carried it to the water while Zabeau Countess tossed the contents of a jar into the river and the water erupted into blue flames.

Shouts of surprise and shock as the worshipers beat the water to extinguish the flames. And quickly as the flames came, they were gone, and the worshipers left the water, dancing and chanting, as they had entered it. Only Aunt Odie and Ruby remained in the river. The naked men and women formed a half circle around Zabeau Countess as she held her arms open for Ruby, but Aunt Odie had to help her from the water; she seemed to be incapable of walking in a straight line. I would have thought she was drunk from the way her legs kicked out from under her and how she twirled her arms.

Zabeau Countess approached, and Ruby yanked away from Aunt Odie and began slapping and scratching at Zabeau Countess's face, but she ignored all that like it was only a minor distraction and took Ruby into her embrace and shouted words from a language I didn't know. Ruby shouted back. She tried to push the witch away, but Zabeau Countess was stronger than she looked and held on like a bull rider and continued to shout those words with all of those people singing and clapping around them.

Even though I was standing far from all this craziness, I felt myself getting carried away with it. Already light-headed and giddy, I heard the drums roar louder and louder till they knocked me off my feet. I hugged the soggy ground, fearing somehow I would be flung off the face of the earth. I saw Ruby on her knees, head hung low, as Zabeau Countess held a cask above her head and poured something upon her, washing her hair with what looked like milk under the full moon overhead. Ruby moaned so loud I could hear her yards away. I crawled toward her on my stomach like a damn snake.

"Lucien, Lucien, come back, you bastard! Come back to me!" Ruby said.

As if Zabeau Countess were trying to wash those words away, she poured more milk over Ruby. And still Ruby pleaded for Lucien to return.

The anger in Zabeau Countess's face! Did she think she could wash away Lucien's grip on Ruby with a couple of gallons of milk? This witch believed in her magic. She readied to pour another cask on her. This was a darkly colored water, thick. I could smell it—the pungent, bittersweet odor of fresh blood.

"Cast this demon out!" Zabeau Countess said.

"Where's Lucien? Ruby asked. "Where's my Lucien?"

Ruby wore Zabeau Countess down. Maybe the

witch was out of tricks. Finally Zabeau Countess gestured for Aunt Odie, and they walked Ruby back out into the water and like Baptists sometimes do, dunked her over and over again till her shouts for Lucien stopped and everything was quiet except for the muted drums.

My father died soon after all the craziness with Zabeau Countess. I heard about his death on the day of the funeral. I didn't know what to do exactly. Being one of his daughters but not being legitimate made it difficult to know my place. His white wife knew of mother and us, but that didn't mean anything. More than likely she would just as soon have us on a slow boat to China. Soon enough a young lawyer showed up with an evil attitude. I didn't care. I signed the paperwork, and I received my inheritance. More than enough money to sell the fish market and take time to think of what to do next, for myself and for Ruby and for the baby, which she named Adele. Ruby gave birth to the child with no problem, and she was truly beautiful, born with an abundance of glorious golden curls and a smile to melt your heart.

Ruby took care of the child well enough, but she didn't seem to truly dote on her as you would expect. She needed to return home to her family, but she never mentioned them. I didn't want to be her guardian any longer, but I had no idea of how to get rid of her. And what really worried me is what would happen to Adele. Then Ruby, who never left the house, was gone, leaving me to wake to the sound of a screaming baby wanting a milk-filled breast.

Later, and after what seemed like a gallon of milk, Ruby returned when the baby was sleeping, without offering a word of explanation of where she had been. I immediately began to suspect that she was up to her old ways. Ruby didn't deserve Adele.

"I found him," she told me as she nursed Adele out on the front porch. She didn't care how much that irritated me, like I was some country fool who didn't know any better.

"Who?" I asked, but I should have known.

"Lucien. He's in Angola."

I held my breath.

"How did you find him?"

"People he know."

"Did you go over there?"

"Oh, yeah. I wanted to see if all that magic of Zabeau Countess would work."

"Did it? You still in love with him?"

Ruby laughed. "No. Man don't mean a thing to me."

"That's good," I said, not believing a word of it.

"I saw him through the fence. No mistaking a good-looking man like that. I yelled to him but I don't think he could see me. Now that I got my shape back, I didn't mind him seeing me."

I couldn't help but shake my head. Thank God they had guards, guns, and dogs—otherwise she would have crawled over whatever to get at him.

"So what are you going to do? Wait on him getting out? Girl, Adele might be grown."

"I ain't studying no Lucien. Like I said, I just wanted to see. Now that I done seen, I'm ready to get back on home to St. Charles."

I didn't want to let on how happy that made me. "You're going back to St. Charles?"

"Oh, yes indeedy. Can't wait to get back to the country."

"Who are you going to stay with? Your mother?"

Ruby laughed. She was truly delighted to be going home.

"Anybody but her. But I got lots of people. Anywhere you go, you gonna run into a Grierson."

"Well, at least let me buy you the train ticket."

Ruby smiled and took my hand.

"You been so good to me. I don't know about all that Zabeau Countess doings, but you've been my guardian angel."

That was sweet of her to say, but I might have felt more kindly seeing her wave good-bye on the next train.

"I don't mean to impose, but I was hoping you could make the trip out to the country with me and the baby. Being how she's already so attached to you. I do know I'm going to need more than a bit of help."

I wanted the baby plain and simple, and I knew I had to convince Ruby to give Adele up to me. It was for Ruby's benefit as well as Adele's; I was the only hope that baby had for a moment's happiness.

"You already done more than your share. If you don't got the time, I understand," Ruby said, staring

right through me. "And don't you fret about it. I done wore out your kindness. I can find my own way home."

"No, you're not. I'm dead set on coming with you."

Ruby stomped with happiness.

"I'll be getting my things together," Ruby said. She hurried to the closet of a room she had been sleeping in and began stuffing her few belongings into a sack.

"Ruby, come here," I said.

"What, the baby woke?"

"No, you can't be going home with all you own in a burlap sack."

"Why? That's how I got out here."

"Because you're supposed to impress them." I led her to my closet and took out a dust-covered valise. "Here, you put your clothes in here."

"I don't need all this for what little I got."

"And you take these, too." I began handing her dresses I hadn't worn in years.

"Why don't you wear these? You got nice clothes.

Most of the time I see you dressing like you don't want a man."

"I don't," I said. "Not right now."

"Some man broke your heart?"

I shrugged. Last thing I wanted to do was talk about my personal matters. Ruby never asked me many questions, just like she didn't answer them.

"Who was the fellah?"

"He was a fisherman, but a storm came up and caught them far out in the gulf. Not one of them made it back to shore."

Ruby listened. Here she was about ready to get out of my hair, and she gets interested in my life story. "Was you engaged?"

"Yes. He was a good man and he was handsome. After him, you know, I just as soon keep my own company."

Ruby smirked as she checked over the dresses I had given her, smoothing the wrinkles and looking at the embroidery. "See, you're different because your family have some money," she said. "Most colored people don't have that. The way we came up, you better find a man straight away. Who's gonna do for you but the man sharing a bed with you? And half the time he don't want to share a nickel with you."

Yes, she was right about that. I didn't need a man to support me. If I had to fight for my daily bread, I don't know what I would do. Still, I'd rather jump into the Mississippi than do the things Ruby did.

"See, I know. You look at me like I'm moldy cheese. I know you don't mean to, but if you could you'd grab a knife and cut off all the rotten parts till there be so little of me you couldn't feed a mouse."

"Don't talk like that. You had some rough going, but I don't hold that against you."

"But you know I messed up and there's nothing I could do about that. That's a cow out the barn."

"Ruby, all you have to do is live a Christian life like you're doing now."

She shrugged as she filled up the valise with Adele's outfits and toys. "Because I'm not working the streets means I'm living like a Christian? Maybe I'm just being lazy because you've been taking care of me."

"Ruby, don't talk that way."

"I'm telling you the truth. God knows I've sinned. Nothing I can do about that."

"You can do penance. Go to confession."

"I ain't baptized by you Catholics, so I'm not going to no confession."

"Why?"

"Who knows? My mama was probably crabbing and didn't want to waste her time. Crabbing, cards, and men, that's the only things she liked. Me, she just wanted to shut up complaining about being hungry."

"Come on, Ruby," I said, and helped her close the valise. Humoring her could wear a person down, but I had to do it, hold my tongue for the baby's sake.

"Come on, what? I ain't lying. That's how it was

in St. Charles. I was hungry, and ain't nobody gave a damn."

"That's why you left?"

"Naw, I left because the best-looking man I ever did see bought me a dress and took me with him."

"Listen, you don't have to go back. If it's that hard, there's no reason."

"There's a reason. Like I said, I done worn out my welcome here and I done worn out my welcome in N'awlins. Time for me go back home, yeah."

It wasn't going to work. She wasn't going to be out of my hair. If she goes home, what then?

"Stay—you have to stay here with me."

She eyed me slyly, rubbing her hands together like squirrels do. "No, couldn't do that. I'd have to pull my weight, yeah. Yes, I would. Wouldn't feel right if I didn't pay you something for me putting you out."

"I won't take your money, but you're welcome to stay here to save for you and the baby."

Ruby beamed, unfastened the valise, and unpacked her things more quickly than I'd ever seen her move.

"Can I still keep these dresses?"

"Yes. I gave them to you."

"You're my guardian angel, that's for sure."

I shrugged, wanting to rip my hair out strand by strand.

✤　✤　✤

I found Ruby a job through some of my father's friends, working as a housekeeper for a rich family in the Garden District. Of course it left me with the baby for hours on end—and the chance to have Adele all to myself was what I wanted. Adele was such a beautiful baby, with bright, big eyes and the prettiest smile. Her coloring was pretty too, like caramel in warm milk. When she called me Mama I didn't tell her to stop, no. And I would have gladly nursed her if I could. I had to expect that everyone would assume someone knocked me up and ran off and there would go my good reputation.

Ruby hadn't been out to that job but a few days before I started to notice how good she looked after a day of cleaning house in the Garden District. When I was out there, those rich white people worked me like a horse heading for the glue factory, trying to get every last drop of sweat before they were through with me. Ruby left for work in those dresses I had given her, and those were good dresses.

One morning after she left for work I followed, with Adele sleeping tight in the new perambulator I had mail-ordered for her. We caught the streetcar across town right after Ruby. There, with Adele sleeping through the getting on and off and the drizzle of the half-cast day, I rolled Adele right up to that great house with the huge oaks on both sides of the porch and with a door so broad and high it made me feel like a child. I rang the bell, wondering if she was there working—but she was. She answered looking like she owned the house and wasn't there to clean and pick up after the children. She was surprised to see me and delighted to see Adele, who had finally awakened. Adele reached with both arms for Ruby, and even though I felt like the child's mother, she knew who her mother really was, and I couldn't help but be jealous.

"What y'all doing coming out to see me all the way over here?"

"Adele was cutting up so much I knew she needed to see you."

Ruby smiled and lifted the baby out of the stroller. "I'm grateful to you. She's a sight for sore eyes."

The way she held her baby, I realized she could be a good mother if she tried.

Ruby brought home a suitor for my approval. Actually, she showed up with two men; one a short, red-faced pig of a white man stuffed into a expensive suit with a gold watch too fat to fit completely into his vest pocket and his hat hung so low over his eyes I wondered how he could see. The other one was colored, and handsome too, though short and slight, dressed well but nowhere near as expensively as the dumpy white man. The colored man was your father. That's how I met him. Ruby looked delighted with these two characters, but I was less than impressed and more suspicious than if a robber with a blackjack had showed up asking for a cup of sugar.

"Helen Murphy, let me introduce you to Marc Boyard and Thomas Du Champ."

"Pleased to meet you," this Thomas said to me. Boyard kissed my hand, which I detest.

"Enchanté," he said.

Ruby looked about to burst with pride. I tried not to roll my eyes and show them the door, but I wondered what chance Ruby would have to find a decent, God-fearing man when all she knew were johns and Lucien.

"Ruby speaks of your beauty, but she does not do you justice." Boyard's eyes bugged wide as he spoke in that heavy French accent.

Thomas stepped forward. "Mr. Boyard is here in New Orleans on business, and he is—"

Before Thomas could finish the sentence, Ruby nudged him aside.

"We're engaged," Ruby said. "To be married!" she continued, like she needed to explain engaged to me.

"Ruby, what are you talking about?"

Ruby didn't answer me because Mr. Boyard was leaning over to whisper into her ear. Thomas cleared his throat. "I work for Mr. Boyard, and he has been looking for a wife. He would like your permission to marry your sister, Ruby."

The repulsive Frenchman smiled and nodded. What kind of marriage was he talking about?

"Mr. Boyard, what do you do?"

He bowed. "I am a buyer and seller of cloth and many such things."

"And why is it that you want a colored bride? You know, in this country people aren't supposed to mix."

"But they do," Thomas said. "They do all the time. Look at yourself."

This Thomas made me want to throttle him. What was he, Mr. Boyard's pimp?

"I, ah . . . lived in the Caribbean for . . . some time." Boyard smiled again, nodding like I should understand what he was getting at. Ruby was grown, and if she wanted to go off with a funny-looking man and be a colored mistress living in some shack on the edge of the town, that was up to her, but men like my father who would take on the responsibilities of two families were gone.

"In this country you can be arrested for marrying a colored. What do you intend to do?"

The Frenchman whispered something to Thomas. He nodded and turned to me like he had the answer. "Mr. Boyard is Canadian, and he plans for them to return to Montreal."

"Oh," I said. I believed him. The way his hand slipped into hers, his ugly lovestruck smile. What kind of man shops around the world looking for brides but a loser? I could see why he was so stuck on Ruby—she was unusually pretty—but there were pretty girls everywhere. I guess he wasn't set in thinking pure whiteness was the only beauty. But this was their business, and I had done enough for her to give me enough grace to last a lifetime.

"What about Adele? You sure you want to take her out of the country?"

"The baby?" the Frenchman asked.

"I'll come back to see her. My niece won't forget me."

Ruby looked at me, her eyes begging me to lie. Adele was mine. Say it. That's all. She was mine.

Ruby was married by a justice of the peace. The justice, a man with such bitter breath I couldn't stand near to him, married them at his office, which was really a shack behind his ramshackle home, and to top it all he was as drunk as a skunk. Maybe they couldn't have found someone else other than a rummy-eyed drunk who married colored people—the Frenchman was now colored in the eyes of our part of the world—but I would have tried a little harder than they did.

Thomas was the best man, and I was the bridesmaid and second witness.

It was done fast, and when "You can kiss the bride" was announced, the Frenchman kissed Ruby so hard it looked like a hungry man sucking down oysters.

I felt it was my duty to cook dinner for them because they were supposed to be sailing for Montreal the following day, but the Frenchman insisted that he cook.

"I cook by profession, and he refuses to let me make him a egg," Thomas said.

The Frenchman nodded proudly. "It's pleasure to cook."

I had begun to doubt that Mr. Boyard had anything to offer the world other than his lopsided smile. I believe he smiled that way to conceal a rotten tooth or two, but Ruby showed me the ring he had gotten for her and I have to admit it was beautiful, so it didn't matter if he had a mouth full of bad teeth. Other than for Adele I've never felt jealousy for anything she had. I did now. All through dinner—goose in some sauce I never tasted before, and fish done up so sweet it tasted like candy, and we all had our own bottle of wine that he thought was so good but was as sour as his odor—she waved her ring around like I hadn't seen it the first dozen times she stuck it under my nose.

I had Adele on my lap because now she was my child, and that was fine, but Adele wasn't in on the plan. She reached for her mother over and over again. Ruby was a good actress and didn't bat an eye or even blink in the child's direction. I had to hold the squirming little thing tight in my arms to keep her from crawling across the table to get at Ruby. Maybe she could smell her milk, and that's what she needed to get at. If I had milk, she wouldn't need Ruby.

I hurried to the kitchen and warmed milk, putting a teaspoon of sugar and a touch of vanilla in it, but still, back at the table, Adele reached for her mother. Finally, I couldn't sit at the table pretending everything was fine and all her mother could do was snuggle up with a butterball of a Frenchman. I rushed her outside, hoping the night air would do her some good. Wrong—she wanted to tear my dress open, but my breast were dry wells, making her all the more unhappy. The door opened behind me. It was Thomas.

"Hello," he said. "Tending to the little one?"

"Trying to," I said.

Thomas stepped close to me and took the squirming child from off my shoulder. "See, I knew she liked men. Stopped crying already."

"How did you know that?"

"I can tell. It's all in the eyes. That's how I work—the eyes have it. Doesn't matter who. Rich white crackers, niggers digging ditches—if you want to know what they want and where they're going, look them in the eye."

I hated this man soon as he started talking. He didn't know me well enough to be so familiar. He looked at me a long time like he had something to say and wanted to wait till just the right time to say it. "I know that's not your baby."

I tried to keep a straight face, not letting on in the least that he had caught me in a lie. "What are you talking about? You don't know anything about me."

He shook his head and made that irritating tsk-tsk noise. "Oh, you can call that baby your own if that's what you want to do."

"I don't think this is any of your business."

"I do get around, and I run errands in the Quarter. And I'm sure I've seen Ruby there, you know, working."

My ears began ringing, and my face flushed. "Listen, you! If you think you are going to get a dime from me, you're dead wrong."

Thomas patted the baby and walked down the steps, and after a bit returned. "I don't care about what's she done. None of my business. I just want to see you happy."

"So why are you telling me this?"

Now it was his turn to squirm. "See, I'm working for this fellah, Mr. Boyard. Most of the time I'm running errands for him and it's okay. Then he decides he needed to get married before he ships out. Crazy, you know. Got me running around all over town introducing him to ladies with just a little coffee in their cream, seeing if they'd want to uproot and go some place like Canada. Nobody I know even knows where it is—'someplace north of the states down here,' they hear—and they don't even want to listen to the offer. He's got money and he wants to marry somebody light brown and beautiful and he wants to treat them like a princess. Maybe if he was a little better-looking—you do got to get past his looks. Some ladies listen to me talk about this white man looking for a colored girl to take home to Canada, and they ask, 'He got money?' I vouch to that fact. He pays me damn well. Then they want to know what he looks like. I can't lie because if they want to meet him and I talk him up saying he looks so good and they see him and want to laugh because he's short and fat with a face like a catfish and a body like a pig, what I'm going to do?"

"You tell them everything, and they still want to see him?" I asked, curiosity getting the best of me.

"Some do. You know, most everybody want to be rich, even if they got to marry somebody who looks like some kind of pig fish. They just don't want to go sailing to someplace they never heard of."

"You work for the man, and here you are telling me all his business."

Thomas laughed. "Oh, I dunno. I like talking to you, and it is your business. That's your sister about ready to take off with him, so I'm just letting you know." He winked at me. "It's funny being paid to be a matchmaker. It's not like being a pimp—not like I know about that. But I'm making good money."

"Good for you. Save some of it."

"You! You got nerve. That's what I like. Pretty

sharp young lady. What do you think of Ruby's ring?"

"It's nice," I said, blasé.

"It cost a fortune. That's all you got to say about it?"

"It's nice. Yes, that's all I got to say about it."

"Oh, well, I'm glad you like it."

Then he reached into his pocket and came out with a small felt box and handed it to me. I tried to hand it back to him, but he slipped out of reach.

"Open it. Take a look at that."

"There's no reason for you to be giving me a present. I can't accept it."

"Just take a look. Tell me what you think of it. I got it for somebody I'm real sweet on, and I just want to make sure it's nice enough."

I sighed and looked at the fancy little box. I guess he wanted me to be jealous—"See, look at the nice ring I'm giving to so-and-so"—but it wasn't going to work.

"Come on! I need your help."

Reluctantly, I opened it. The ring in there was beautiful, a huge glittering stone and a band with the most elaborate and delicate design. Just as nice as the one Ruby had. "It's beautiful. How can you afford this?"

"I work hard seven days a week."

"Unless you're rich, I don't see how you paid for this."

"Try it on."

"No, this is for your fiancée. She's the one who should try it on."

"But I want you to try it."

"No, we're not engaged. We're nothing. I don't need to try it on."

He frowned and dropped to one knee. "Don't make me do this."

"I'm not making you do anything," I said.

He stood up and took my hand. "You need to marry me."

"No, I don't."

"No, I need to marry you."

"No, you don't," I said.

He stood and shrugged like a beaten man. "Okay, you won't marry me?"

"No, I won't."

He sighed, then started down the street.

"Here! Come get your ring."

"No, you keep it for me. Try it on. You might change your mind," he said.

"Be a cold day in hell."

He laughed as he walked away.

Within days Ruby would be gone from my life. She'd sail away with Mr. Boyard to some new life in Montreal with all the excitement of a child going to the circus. I dreaded the parting because of Adele. Since Ruby had given up any obligation of motherhood to me, the child was either listless or colic. It hurt me to hear her whimpering for Ruby as I tried my best to soothe her. There at the dock, Ruby was splendid in a blue silk brocade dress the Frenchman had bought for her from the most expensive shop in the Quarter. Ruby had managed to tell me how much it cost and all that at least a half dozen times since she showed it to me the night before.

People were rushing by us to board, so I missed seeing Thomas walk up beside me, grinning like a Cheshire cat as I waited for the final farewells. I hope he didn't expect to console his way to my affections. I couldn't take my eyes off Ruby, primping and posing like a movie idol, doing all she could to make the Frenchman drool. The squirming, wailing girl reached for her again and again, but Ruby deftly managed to ignore most of Adele's demands, turning at awkward angles to keep someone between the baby and her. Finally the whistle blew for the passengers to board. Ruby reached for the baby for the final time and held her like she meant it. Brought tears to my eyes seeing that child look overjoyed to be in her mother's arms. Even being the actress she was, Ruby couldn't pull it off without a tear, specially when the child wouldn't let go. Little hands wouldn't release Ruby's hair and blouse, until I pried them loose. We all were sobbing and crying to the point where the Frenchmen started to shout at Adele in his native tongue.

"Last call to board!" a steward called.

The Frenchman led Ruby away, and I was sick to my stomach watching her go. It wasn't right to take a child from her mother, even if I had good reason.

Adele was no longer colicky, just listless to the point that I called Dr. Mouton, and he hurried over. The exam didn't take long, but the minutes inched by with me biting my nails to the quick.

He came out of the bedroom grim-faced, carrying no news I would want to hear. "She isn't thriving. Maybe it's your milk."

"I'm not nursing."

"You're not?"

"No," I said, shaking my head. "I'm the mother, but she's not my own. My cousin couldn't afford another child, so I took her in."

Dr. Mouton rubbed the thinning gray hairs on his head. "That explains it."

"What, doctor?"

Dr. Mouton shook his head again. "Infants just have a rough time when they separate from their birth mother. Some don't make it."

That's all I heard him say, and it was enough to make me collapse onto the couch. Dr. Mouton did his best to comfort me, but even two shots of whiskey didn't calm me. Nothing could happen to that girl. It would kill me as surely as a knife through the heart.

❖   ❖   ❖

Aunt Odie came soon after I called her, and though she brought Zabeau Countess, again from head to toe in the whitest sheets, I was happy to see the both of them. Voodoo or what, I just wanted somebody to help my child. She was wasting away; I had to struggle to get her to take a sip of water. Zabeau Countess headed straight for the crib without so much as a nod to me. She didn't touch the baby, just looked down at the whining thing and shook her head.

"What?" I shouted.

Aunt Odie gestured for me to wait.

Zabeau Countess turned to us, her arms stretched out to the sky, and her eyes rolled up into her head. I swear to God the voice she spoke in wasn't her own. A deep baritone of a very big man came from somewhere within her.

"UNBELIEVER!"

I landed on my knees like a hurricane blew me down.

"HEAR MY WORDS! YOU DOUBTED AND NOW YOU SEE!"

Zabeau Countess finished shouting and collapsed onto the floor next to me. Whatever spell she had me under lifted. I ran for the baby and scooped her from the crib and clasped her to my chest.

"Save her!"

The little woman's steely eyes fixed on me. "You trust me now, but it might be too late. I will do what I can."

She pointed to a chair, and I sat and watched her and Aunt Odie make their preparations. I saw Aunt Odie in the kitchen working at the kitchen table grating bits of root until she had a small mound, which she carefully scooped up and dropped into a pot of water boiling on the stove.

Zabeau Countess set up various colored candles and lit them and prayed over each flame. From a bottle she poured water into a small wooden bowl and placed it by the door, then she opened a jar of something that looked like lard but smelled awful, almost brought tears to my eyes.

"You're going to use that on her?"

Zabeau Countess looked at me with so much contempt I would have run out of the room, except I couldn't bear to leave Adele. The witch took a handful of the poultice and walked over to the baby, who must have smelled the evil concoction. She began wailing like she hadn't in days.

"Don't be afraid, little one," she said, smearing Adele from foot to head with the foul stuff.

"You think it could help?" I found myself shouting, knowing I wouldn't get an answer that would make me breathe any easier.

The room also filled up with the suffocating smell of those scented candles and a new odor, bitter and piercing, those roots boiling on the stove. "You're not going to give that to her," I said to Aunt Odie, but she wouldn't even look at me. Zabeau

Countess turned and, with her eyes flaring, pointed to the door.

"Go!"

"I can't go. I need to be here —"

"You are not helping. You distract me from what I need to do," Zabeau Countess said.

Against my better judgment I headed for the door. "When will you know something?" I asked, but they both ignored me as they put together their witch's brew.

They could kill her doing that mumbo-jumbo, but I didn't have a choice. She was getting too weak to hold on. I walked back and forth on the porch, forcing myself to wait a few minutes before going back in to see if they made progress or if they made things worse.

Worrying, going in circles like a crazy, caged dog, and most of all, breathing so quickly, I became too light-headed to stand. I sat on the steps of the porch, put my head below my knees, and tried to stop my head from spinning. I guess maybe I passed out, because I woke with a start.

I turned to look into the face of Zabeau Countess.

"I appealed to the Loa, and he has been generous."

"What?" I said.

"You have been given a reprieve. She won't be taken from you."

This woman's words, this witch's words, carried
me to such heights of relief. I rushed inside to see, but
there she was in the crib looking as pathetic as when
I left—worse, because that medicine or poison, whatever, had her whimpering.

"She's no different! She looks worse than
before."

136

Aunt Odie came over and put a wet cloth on the
baby's head, but she didn't answer. Instead, she nodded at the witch. "She'll explain."

Zabeau Countess waited with her hand outstretched for me to take hold of. I did and she gazed
at me, trying to look into my eyes, but I shifted about.
She made me feel like a frog waiting to be eaten by a
snake. Finally she caught me with her eyes. "You will
be given a sign. A dark horse will bring the end of her
suffering."

"A horse? I don't know anything about horses."

"A sign. The horse brings a sign."

"When! She can't take much more of this."

"Whenever the Loa decides."

"Out! Out! Take all of this garbage and get out
of my house."

My rage caught Zabeau Countess square in the
face. She stumbled backward away from me. Aunt
Odie rushed over to hold and comfort her and to protect if I did get after her.

"Apologize to Zabeau Countess," Aunt Odie said.

"No, I won't. You two are supposed to help me,

but you're no help. The baby looks worse. Neither of you have a clue about what you're doing."

Zabeau Countess pulled herself away from Aunt Odie and began gathering all her belongings. Aunt Odie shook her head and looked at me with pity. "You don't know. You've turned your back on the one woman who tried to help."

"Oh, there's nothing you can do for this one. She doesn't believe. And she won't believe."

The madness faded, and I was just sad and tired. It didn't matter if I screamed till my lungs burst. Adele, my baby, was going to die. I couldn't bear to think those words, but I couldn't deny them any longer.

Zabeau Countess warily stepped forward, watching me, unsure of what I might do. "The baby will live, but her life will not be sweet and neither will yours," she said coldly. Her words didn't move me at all. I was no longer desperate enough to believe this witch one way or the other.

Zabeau Countess waved for Aunt Odie to hurry along with her things. Once she had all the candles and bowls and the rest of it, they stood at the door looking at me.

"Go, if you're going," I said, and watched them turn their backs on me.

We were alone, and I held onto Adele as if a sickly baby could keep me afloat.

❁ ❁ ❁

I slept with the baby on my chest and had troubled dreams of a tight space; a box, a coffin, with water seeping in and my hands bloody and useless, but still they scratched at the lid of what held me.

I woke to what I thought was the booming of my heart. Someone was banging at the door hard enough to wake the dead. I left it unanswered because I couldn't take my eyes off my girl. For the last few weeks loud noises or piano music or sweet cakes couldn't shake Adele from the torpor, but here she sat bolt upright staring at the door like she expected Ruby to be on the other side.

The pounding continued, but anybody who couldn't knock in a civilized manner didn't need to set foot in my house. Adele didn't agree. Squirming mightily, she did her best to crawl toward the door. "Is that somebody you want to see?" I asked her, but a six-month-old baby didn't have words to say.

Then she screamed as loud as I ever heard her, stopping only when I scooped her up and let her peek through the curtain.

"Hello, Thomas," I said sharply as I opened the door. "Just why are you pounding on my door like a crazy man?"

First time I could remember seeing him without a silly smile. He looked relieved to see us. "I was on my way over here to see how you were doing. I been meaning to check in on you. I saw your aunt walking with that witch woman. She told me you were in a bad way and you'd be expecting me. I got here and nobody answered and I got worried."

"Worried about what?"

"About you and the baby. You know, I might run the streets but I got a heart. I worried about you being all on your own without a man to lean on and all."

"No need to be worried about me. I take care of myself," I said.

Adele just about flung herself into his arms, and he had sense enough to catch her.

"How's your girl? Looks a little thinner than when I last saw her."

I sighed. "Yes. She hasn't been doing very well."

Adele crawled up his shoulder, sucking at his neck like it was a nipple.

"Oh, whoa! Go get this girl a bottle, quick!"

Excited to see her wanting milk again, I rushed into the house and grabbed that bottle I had been try-ing to coax her to drink with little success and got it to him as quickly as I could.

"Oh, yeah. This one's hungry."

Adele snatched the rubber nipple into her mouth and lustily drank to the last drop. She held it out, waving for more.

I fetched her two bottles more before she fell into an exhausted sleep.

"See, I told you I'm good with children. You just have to have the touch."

I looked at his hands. He had very handsome hands.

"Listen. I'm not giving up on you. So when you gonna say yes?"

"To what?"

"Don't you play dumb. I want you to be my wife. Adele's gonna need some brothers and sisters."

"Listen you, I appreciate you coming over and helping me with the girl, but I'm not ready to be married. I've had hard luck, and I don't know when I'll feel up to chancing it again."

He sighed and sat down on the porch, stroking Adele's hair.

"So, you saying you don't want to marry me?"

"No."

"Swell. I'm loving a women who can't stand me."

"I didn't say that."

"But that's what you mean."

"Let me make you dinner."

That made him brighten. He popped up and gave a bow. "Thank you."

"You deserve a dinner for all the trouble you've had to go through."

Thomas did a little dance, twirling with the sleeping baby around the broad porch. "I knew you'd come around. See me for the good guy I am. That's how I am. I stay in the race when most horses would have quit and gone back to the barn."

Adele was going to make it. Come what may, my little girl was going to make it.

Finished, Mother sighed, struggling to catch her breath. Tears rolled freely down her cheeks.

"I never told Adele about Ruby, and I certainly didn't tell her about Lucien. I don't want her to know. That kind of knowledge just eats you up. I've been hard on you because I wanted you to have the strength to survive. With Adele it was always borrowed time."

Drained of energy, Mother had to be helped to her room. Once she was settled, she fell into a deep sleep. Me, I was wide awake for the rest of the night, thinking of my sister, wondering if she was alive or dead, as Mother thought.

The next morning Father Fitzpatrick showed up a little late to Saint Katherine's and a little drunk, but he was in fine form and made me laugh more than I thought I could. Even Winston seemed to loosen up when Father reminded him to salute. Father Fitzpatrick served as a chaplain in England during the First World War, and he didn't want anyone to forget. Now he was the priest of one of the colored churches, and he seemed to truly enjoy himself at the weddings and funerals; after mass you'd see him with a plate of food in one hand and a good stiff drink in the other, having more fun than a priest probably should in public, but nobody minded if he got flat-out drunk and made a pass at somebody. He was our priest. People talked about the time he slugged it out with Father Murphy at the downtown church because Father Murphy wouldn't even let colored people sit in the last two pews, as is the custom in most white churches. He said Negroes could go to hell, and not even the pope could make him let them into his church. When Father Fitzpatrick heard about what Father Murphy said, he called Father Murphy out, right there on the steps of the church straight after mass. They had a knock-down, drag-out right there. Next Sunday he came back telling everybody how he had to beat the Irish into Father Murphy for his own good.

Mother watched us from the first row of pews as we practiced the wedding march. She looked happier than I seen her look in a long time as Father Fitzpatrick pulled us about the altar, positioning us just so. Daddy shifted from leg to leg as he stood next to me. Then I heard Mother gasp, and there was Adele in her brides-maid's gown, looking like a million dollars. I don't know if I had ever been more relieved to see anybody in my life. Daddy and the twins rushed to her, and Adele held onto them like a drowning man grasping for shore.

Father Fitzpatrick was busy reading from something in Latin, explaining it for us, so engrossed that he didn't notice the reunion and all the crying and laughing. Adele saw Mother heading to the exit, and she yanked free of Ana and Ava and rushed over to her. At first I was paralyzed, with no idea of what to do, but I knew Adele chasing Mother down was going to make things worse. "Excuse me, Father, but I've got to speak to my sister," I said, and raced after Adele, grabbing hold of her just as she was about to reach Mother.

"No, you stay," I said, and shoved her back toward the rehearsal. I caught up with Mother just as she stepped outside into the bright spring afternoon. "You can't just leave—you're not being fair to me," I said.

Mother looked subdued. "Send her away, or I'm leaving."

"Why are you doing this? Talk to her. Maybe now she'll listen to you."

Mother sighed, looking tired and ghostly pale. "Adele isn't the kind to listen. If she listened, she wouldn't have stayed with that bastard in the first place." Her voice was just above a whisper.

"So you're going to pretend she's dead even though she's looking you in the face. What kind of sense does that make?"

"You don't understand."

"I understand. You just want to break her because she didn't listen to you."

Mother's eyes hardened and she raised her hand, but she stopped mid-swing. Then she turned her back to me and resumed walking in the direction of home, muttering. "I can't take it," she said. "I'm not going through it again."

"Going through what?"

Mother looked surprised to see me there, like she forgot I was standing at her shoulder. "She's killed herself," she said.

"No, she hasn't. She's as alive as we are."

"No, she's not," Mother said, and found a bench to sit down on.

"What are you talking about?"

"She's done. It's over for her."

I didn't have a clue to what Mother was talking about, and I certainly didn't know what to do. I felt like just walking home and saying, "The hell with all of them." Then I saw the doors of the church swing outward and Adele came bursting through, looking wildly about for a second and then seeing Mother. She ran over and dropped to her knees and buried her face in Mother's lap.

Mother sat there like stone, as though Adele wasn't even there.

Adele lifted her head. I figured she was all cried out, but I was wrong. "It's over! I'm sorry," she said, and she began to wail, and it went on and on. Until Mother broke down and began crying too, matching Adele's wail in every way. Everyone inside the church came out to see. Father Fitzpatrick pulled Adele up and led her and Mother into the church, where they would talk for so long Winston and I had to walk the girls home for bed.

"She's back," I said to Winston. "I told you."

"That's something," he said. "But I don't think it means anything."

"It means something; it means she's come to her senses, and if you're not happy to see her, you ought to pretend, because she's still a good person who loves her family, who loves me."

"I didn't say a darn thing. Don't go getting mad at me." Winston shrugged like he really didn't mean to make me want to knock him upside the head. Anyway, I needed him to carry Ana. Knocked out, he wouldn't be any good at all.

*H*ome, *Adele collapsed* onto my narrow bed that used to be her narrow bed, in the bedroom that used to be hers but was now mine for the next few days. Then Ava and Ana could fight for a six-by-six, windowless closet of a bedroom. Adele wouldn't talk about how she and Mother had reconciled, but they had. Mother seemed relieved and at ease with Adele, and till

Mother fell asleep she had her hands in Adele's hair, combing and braiding, brushing and oiling her scalp like she did the twins. She had her baby back. Wherever Adele had gone or whatever she had done, Mother had nothing to say about it and neither did Adele.

Once Adele had slowed down, the giddiness of reunion was replaced with exhaustion and wariness, as though she expected me to annoy her with questions about where she had gone or what had happened. I didn't need to ask anything. I knew she was with Lucien. I handed Adele her mail but held the letter from Rene till last. Sighing, she tore the weathered envelope open. Grim news, I thought, but Adele smiled and folded the paper and slipped it into her bosom. She took it better than I thought she would, even better than when I told her about the dead cat I found in her kitchen.

"Rene, he's a good man," she said.

"He is?" I asked. "What did Rene say?"

She laughed. "Read it yourself," she said, retrieving it from her cleavage and handing it to me.

The letter was very short, written in a sad scrawl.

Dear Adele:

I forgive you. Please come home.
I'll wait on you forever.

—Love, Rene.

I couldn't say I wasn't shocked. Rene was a good man or a very stupid one, maybe even both.

"So are you going to go back and start again with Rene?"

Adele rolled her eyes. "I'm a married woman. What else am I supposed to do?"

I shrugged.

"I know I've been bad, but now I'm ready to make it up to Rene. Make it up to everybody."

147

"You don't have to do nothing for me. I'm just glad you're home."

Adele picked up a mirror and examined her face, particularly a discoloration under her right eye. I wondered if she'd used her talent for makeup to conceal the last traces of a beating.

"What did you all think happen to me?" she asked.

I shrugged. "I . . . just worried about you."

"You thought I was dead," she said, calmly.

"I didn't believe that. I knew you were okay."

Adele smiled and copped me on the head with the brush. "How would you know? I was gone. Daddy told me how hard you were looking to find me."

I snatched the brush from Adele and copped her on the knee with it. "Even," I said.

"I know you want to know. I know how Mother was sure I was gone for good. See, you don't understand how I do things. I do them my own way. I told Lucien I was leaving him, and he wanted me to see if he could change my mind. Took me on a little tour

down to Florida, but I had my mind made up, no matter how sweet he was, he couldn't change it."

"Where is he now?"

"I don't know. Maybe still in Florida."

Adele closed her eyes and sat perfectly still, like
she was saying a prayer.

It had to be like that. So last-minute that even
though I swore I wouldn't let it get to me, it did. I
hoped Mother would handle it. She said she could
handle Aunt Dot, but it turned out she couldn't, not
anymore. It was up to me to get my own wedding
dress on the eve of my wedding from Aunt Dot, who
for whatever greedy and stupid notion now pro-
claimed she needed twice the agreed-to money before
she'd turn it over. Mother was outraged; so was
Adele. Daddy said he was outraged but had too much
going on to go over and give that crazy woman what
she deserved.

It was up to me, but I don't know if I was up to
Aunt Dot.

"I'll go with you," Adele said, as I reluctantly
headed for the door.

"Mother's resting. Who'll watch the kids?"

Ava and Ana sat huddled in front of the radio, listening to *Suspense,* but we had enough right there in the
living room.

"Let them stay. They won't get into no mischief if they're listening to that radio."

I was grateful for Adele volunteering to come with me. Going to Aunt Dot's alone was tough enough, but this dress thing would get ugly. I just knew it. We were almost out the door when I thought about Richie. I suspected Richie had no interest in returning home. He hadn't mentioned Aunt Dot in the time he had been staying with us. Mother had tired herself out supervising the hanging of decorations, and even though the boy was quiet and dutiful as a dog, around her he wouldn't do a damn thing Daddy asked. I didn't think it was a good idea to have him there to get in Daddy's way when Daddy was being useful getting the wedding together. He hadn't warmed to the boy, and I don't think he had any patience for him, just another mouth eating off of Mother's hard work.

"You trying to get rid of me," Richie said, when I told him I wanted him to come with us to visit his mother. The boy pulled away and ran to Mother's room, where he slid headfirst under the bed like a roach disappearing into a crack.

I squatted down and called to him in my sweetest voice. "Richie, you don't have to stay. You can come back over here with us. You've got a home here as long as you want."

"I ain't going nowhere," he said, with mannish authority, not like an eight-year-old. "I'm staying here with Auntie Helen."

I thought about bending down and dragging him out of there, but I knew it would be like wrestling with a cornered rat.

"Stay here, but stay out of my daddy's hair."

"Yeah, okay, Cousin Lita. You can count on me." He stuck his head out from under the bed and said, "Thanks," and for a second I had a clean shot at nabbing him, but I let him return to his lair. I don't know. If we were all gone from the house, Mother, Daddy, me and Adele and the girls, even if the house was blown away in some hurricane, he'd be under that bed.

Adele drove Daddy's car like she was crazy or drunk, cutting in front of cars and running lights. I screamed and almost pissed myself when she charged ahead of a streetcar and bolted across its path so close I saw the conductor cover his eyes.

"You're trying to kill us!"

Adele grinned. "Little excitement, yeah. What's wrong with that?"

"I don't need excitement. I need my dress, not you killing me the day before the wedding."

"See, you don't remember this, but Mother once had to hog-tie Aunt Dot over some silverware of Grandmother Bing," Adele said, relishing the memory.

"Mother hog-tied her?"

"Oh, yeah, but that was after Aunt Dot hit her in

the head with the serving tray. Dropped Mother to her knees, but she came to and took off her belt and whipped that Dot good, and then she tied her arms and legs together and left her like a trussed-up cow."

I guess I was supposed to believe that, but it seemed damned silly. "You saw all this?"

"Oh, yeah. Daddy was there too. He was holding me the entire time they were fighting."

Then it was true. Too much like him to be made up. Amazing Daddy didn't sell tickets to the main event.

"Mother and Aunt Dot always hated each other. Every now and then they get together for family business and throw salt into each other's eyes. That's how they are," Adele said, and now here we were, for round two of a tag-team match. Mother was out, so now it was our turn.

I knocked at the door with Adele standing on one side so Aunt Dot wouldn't be able to see her. Adele had the idea that if she saw too many of our family she might not even open the door, suspecting a full-scale feud.

I knocked again, yelled, and screamed, "AUNT Dot!" but still no response. The day before the wedding, and no wedding dress. She had to have it in there somewhere. "Adele, nobody's home," I said, near tears.

"We've got to break in."

"Break in?"

"Look, we don't have no choice."

Adele walked around to the side of the house, testing windows. She found an open one at shoulder level.

"Here! I'll go open the door," she said, and even though she had on a skirt, she shimmied through the open window like she was born swimming upstream. Minutes later, the door opened, and there was a smiling Adele. She looked giddy to have gotten away with something.

I surveyed Aunt Dot's immaculate house.

"Where should we look?" Adele asked me.

I shrugged.

Adele led the way, and I followed her like a hopeless child.

"You been in here?" Adele asked. "You know she never lets anybody but her kids go past the kitchen."

"No, not me," I said, as Adele opened the swinging doors of the kitchen.

I swear to God some wild animal came bursting out of that room.

Aunt Dot sprang from behind the door with her brood behind her. Both of her biggest boys, Albert Jr. and Sonny, looked ready to do some bloodletting. Albert was a big ten-year-old, missing teeth and battle-scarred, and Sonny was fat as a short-legged hog, a minor miracle in itself since she kept all of them on half rations. Also, that boy had fingernails like a vampire.

Goes to show what kind of crazy fool Aunt Dot was to let a boy get away with something like that.

"Now, what y'all sneaking around my house for?" Aunt Dot gripped a thick club, and her boys were grinning like little monsters licking their chops.

"We came for the dress," I said.

My words enraged her, and she took a step toward me. "You ain't seeing a thing till I get fifty dollars. Took me twice as long to do that work, so I need to be paid."

I sighed. "Look, Aunt Dot, I don't mean to be disrespectful, but we had a deal—"

"Disrespectful my ass! I got the damn dress, and unless you come across with some more money, I'm gonna be cutting it up for rags."

Adele pushed me aside. Aunt Dot smirked. "Now, don't you supposed to be run off from your husband or something?"

Adele shook her head, smiling. "Aunt Dot, you know she's getting married tomorrow, and we can't leave without it."

"Oh, if you don't give me fifty dollars it'll be over your dead body. And I really don't care if you got hot pants for anything with balls. You know, I always liked you, you was my favorite of Helen's kids because you don't act stuck-up like Lita here, even if you ain't a real Du Champ," Aunt Dot said, like she had really stung Adele. But Adele just laughed and opened her purse and came out with a fat wad of fresh bills. I could tell Adele was burning up about Aunt Dot saying she wasn't a real Du Champ, but she could keep a poker face when she wanted.

"Let's see that dress," Adele said, and Aunt Dot smiled like we were her favorite nieces in the whole wide world and she hadn't threatened to bludgeon us over fifty dollars.

Soon as she hurried away to find the dress, the little boys, Albert and Sonny, relaxed and smiled at us. "You got candy?" the fat one asked. I shook my head, but Adele came up with a mint. "That's it? I'm some hungry, yeah."

Adele gave him another one. Then Aunt Dot returned with the dress cradled in her arms, smiling like she was eloping with it. She held it up in front of me, and for a moment she seemed to be a seamstress interested in the quality of her work. "Oh, yeah. You gonna look some good in this. Worth every penny you paid."

"But I don't know about twice as many pennies," I said.

She cut her eyes. "See, that's why me and your mother don't get along. She's always got something to say."

"Excuse me, Aunt Dot, but I think Lita should try on the dress."

"She ain't trying on a damn thing until I get some money."

Adele counted off twenty dollars.

"Now if the dress don't need alterations, I'll give you the rest."

Aunt Dot looked us over like we were about to steal her firstborn, but I don't think she would've minded giving us her firstborn if she could've made a profit.

"Go on, Lita," said Adele. "You go change."

I headed for the bathroom with Sonny the fat boy following me. I tried to shoo him away from the door, but he just grinned and ignored me. I shut the door in his face so hard that he stepped back, cowering.

I'll remember that bathroom. Everything gleamed, from the porcelain of the toilet and the tub to the glass doorknobs. Then I noticed the lack of toilet paper or towels. A show bathroom.

I wiggled into the wedding dress, and instantly I knew it fit me better than anything I had ever worn. I looked into the shining bathroom mirror. Even with my hair looking as bad as Aunt Dot's, I felt like a million dollars. It was worth it. All of this trouble with crazy, lunatic relatives . . . it was worth it.

I returned to them with Sonny, shadowing me, making sure I wouldn't throw myself out of a window and hightail it home in a wedding dress.

"You look pretty as a picture," Aunt Dot said, as though she meant it.

"Really, even prettier than any picture. I'm proud to have a baby sister who looks so good." Adele slipped her arm around my waist and led me to the door. "Go!" she whispered, shoving Daddy's car keys into my hand. She opened the front door and pushed me outside as I heard Aunt Dot screaming bloody murder. Adele almost knocked me down as she slammed the door behind her. Then she stopped and held onto the handle, one of those long brass jobs.

"Go!" she said.

Adele struggled to hold the handle with all the strength in her small body as Aunt Dot tried to yank it open. I hiked the wedding dress up and ran back to the porch, but she waved me off. "Lita! Start the damn car!"

Then I saw Albert Jr. come running from along the side of the house, charging like a freight train. Adele heard him coming, turned, and slashed at him with her purse, which caught him on the side of that big, thick head. That purse hit him like a brick—in fact Adele kept a brick in there, just for this kind of occasion. The boy yelped and slammed hard onto the ground. I thought we were home free, but then the door swung open behind Adele, and she had to run for it. Aunt Dot and Sonny were biting at her heels. I didn't want to have any part of Aunt Dot's bat. I started Daddy's car and shoved the passenger door open for Adele. She leaped in, slammed the door shut as I gunned the engine, and shifted into drive, but not before Aunt Dot took a swing and smashed the passenger window. Glass exploded down on Adele. She screamed, and I stopped the car in shock. That's when I caught a glimpse of Sonny's hand darting into the window and raking my face with his devil nails. Damn! He caught me good.

Boom!

Aunt Dot beat against the already smashed side door, trying to whack Adele.

"GO!" Adele shouted.

I burned rubber away, hot blood running down my cheek.

What was that about?" I said, my hand pressed against the deep gashes that little bastard dug into my cheek, but Adele didn't answer. She was too busy giggling and picking shards of glass off her lap and tossing them out onto the road.

"What are you laughing at!" I shouted, but that just made her laugh more.

"Lita, you pull over," she said, finding the wind to respond. I did, and she rushed around to my side of the car and led me from it.

"Hold this," she said and handed me a silk scarf.

"Did blood get on the dress!" I shouted.

Adele examined the dress as best she could by dim streetlight. "No, I don't think so."

"It's a miracle."

Then Adele nudged me into the backseat and slipped into the driver's seat. Even in the poor light I saw blood trickling along the side of her face.

"But you're bleeding too."

"It's just a little cut on my scalp. Nothing to worry about, no."

She drove for a few miles, and I didn't realize where we were until she stopped. "Let's go home! Not here."

Adele laughed. "You want to kill Mother? If she saw you and me bleeding like pigs the day before your wedding, she'd die right there."

"But we can go to Winston. I'm sure he's got bandages—"

"Don't you know he ain't going to understand? You just going to make him feel crazy for marrying you. Might even make him think you more like me than you know."

I shrugged. "What was Aunt Dot talking about, you not being a real Du Champ?" I asked.

Adele sighed. "Figured it out, huh? You know, it's amazing how long everybody kept it a secret. I'm not Mother's child. She took me in. Mother didn't tell me at first. Aunt Dot did, but she don't know no more than that. If she knew who my real parents were, she would have held it over my head like an ax."

"Mother holds secrets," I said. Obviously Mother never told her about Ruby or Lucien. She was still in the dark, and I couldn't bring myself to tell her about how Lucien treated her real mother.

"She thought she was protecting me, keeping me from being hurt by the truth. Just like with Lucien, she thinks she knows what's best. But what's gonna happen is gonna happen. I never worry about those kind of things. I can't live that way."

"Maybe Mother was worried you might not love her the same way if she told you."

Adele sighed. "Mother is my only mother, Daddy is my father. Whoever those people who had me, they don't have me now."

I followed Adele through that dark, overrun back-yard, expecting anything. We reached the porch and my heart began to pound so hard I imagined Adele or anyone else in earshot could hear it. Maybe she was fearless. That's what I came to believe—that she got herself in such crazy situations because she didn't have sense enough to be afraid. She was so sure of herself, so sure that there was nothing to fear. She went on inside and I didn't want to be outside, alone, bleeding, so I followed her inside. The house was dark as a tomb, and it smelled like one, because of the dead cat.

Adele gagged, and for the first time tonight she seemed at a loss for what to do, arms folded around herself, leaning against the sink, crying to herself.

"Is that Blackie?" she asked.

"Yeah, I should have buried him, but I—"

Then she cried. I felt bad for her, but she wouldn't let me hold her. Instead she rifled through some kitchen drawers, tossing things to the floor until she found what she wanted: candles and matches. "Where is he?" she asked, in a strained and broken voice.

"Over there," I said, pointing to the oven.

"First I'll fix you up, then I'm going to take care of him."

Adele led me through the dark house, lighting candles in each room. In the bathroom she found gauze and medical cream and began doctoring my face.

"Once we stop the bleeding," she said, "we can do some things to keep it from scarring."

"What about tomorrow?"

"Don't you worry. Makeup. Makeup will hide most things. I know all about it. It'll work. Believe me." After she thoroughly cleaned the wound, she went about taping slivers of gauze to my face. "See, tomorrow nobody's going to notice these cuts. I'll see to that." Then Adele turned from me, the smile evaporated from her face. "I got to bury him," she said.

We looked around the house but couldn't find anything to dig a hole but a soup spoon.

"This'll have to do," she said, squatting down to scoop up the dead cat in a towel and carry him into the backyard, where she knelt down a few feet from the steps and began digging in the soft earth.

"You're watching me bury this sad little cat in your wedding dress. It just has to be bad luck."

I wasn't going back into the house, and she was just about through covering the hole, so I figured I'd just ignore her, but Adele was stubborn. She refused to finish. Better to give in than stay longer, so I retreated to the threshold of the back door. Adele finished making a burial mound, and then she prayed over the cat's grave. I wondered how long this would go on: then headlights swept through, illuminating the kitchen. The lights cut, and I heard the sound of a car door slamming.

Adele noticed too and ran to the porch and pulled me to the old Packard. We both crouched behind it as we saw a flashlight bobbing around the house.

"Who's that?" I asked.

Adele just exhaled. "You stay. Don't follow me. Just stay right here, little sister. Promise me."

I was too scared to do anything but nod.

Adele walked to the house like she didn't have a care. She was going in there maybe for Lucien to hurt her or worse because of me: because of the dress, because of the wedding, because she thought she needed to protect me.

No. I wouldn't listen to her. It wasn't a promise I could keep.

I followed her inside. I don't know what I expected except for voices: the sound of Adele begging Lucien for her life, for my life. I heard nothing but the sound of a quiet house.

"She's not here!" I heard Adele say from the distance of a few rooms.

"Where is she?" Somebody responded. It wasn't Lucien's deep, shit-stained, honey-toned voice. I heard Winston.

I felt like charging in on them and throwing myself into his arms, but something urged me to hold back.

"What are you doing here?" Winston asked, but it was more of a challenge than a question.

"I live here. It's my house."

Winston snorted. "No lights, no water, no gas, whatever you doing, you ain't living here. You staying with your Mother. Now, where's Lita? The twins said you left together."

"I dropped her off at her girlfriend's."

"Which girlfriend? Where?"

Adele started to laugh, bitterly like she does when she's about to explode.

"See, you're not good for Lita. She listens to you. That's the last thing she needs to be doing," he said.

"How would you know?" Adele said, and something else, but I couldn't make that out.

"Women like you," Winston said, in almost a shout. "You're the ones who—"

"Go home! You'll find her there. Don't worry. You'll see her, snug as a bug in a rug."

"That's great. I hope you're right. I hope you don't mess up her life like you messed up your own."

"Please, go find your fiancée. I'm sure she's expecting you."

I heard Winston's heavy steps heading for the door, but then he stopped. "You better come on back to your mother's."

"Don't you worry about me, no. You go see about Lita."

I heard the door open.

"By the way, is that your daddy's car? What the hell happened to it? Looks like somebody took a bat to it."

"I dunno. You'll have to ask him."

Finally he left. The car started, and the headlights streamed through the kitchen as Winston rolled away. I felt confused. Even though I was glad he was worried for me, I didn't like the way he lit into Adele like that. I just wanted him to leave my family out of his mind. I walked into the living room, calling for Adele. "Let's go. Let's get the hell out of here."

Adele laughed. "Not before we get you out of that wedding dress. Find something for you to wear so you don't end up bleeding all over it."

I nodded and waited and she returned with some kind of smock that only pregnant women wore.

"Where did you get something like this?" I said. "Couldn't be more ugly."

"Just get out of the dress and slip this on. Too bad about your clothes at Aunt Dot's. Be glad I grabbed your purse. She was about to go for mine. Imagine getting robbed by your aunt! That's the kind of thing gets people talking about you and you can't live it down."

I shook my head, feeling sick to my stomach.

We left the house, and now that I was calmer and relieved to be leaving this last stop of one bad night, I saw the damage to Daddy's car. He tried to keep that Plymouth cherry, but it wasn't cherry no more. I shook my head as I inspected the door.

Adele snorted. "What are you worried about? Daddy'll have one of his drunks put in a new window and knock out those dents in no time, and he'll pay them with a few bottles of that shitty whiskey."

I knew she was right. Daddy didn't deserve consideration. I almost sat on the shattered glass in the front seat.

"Little sister, watch your behind. I'm sure Winston don't want nothing to happen to that."

"Mind your own business," I said.

Adele dropped me off a bit before she reached our door, and I entered the house through the front instead of through the bar. I figured Winston would be waiting for me there. After being out on some crazy mission, stepping into a house in the middle of wedding preparations was one big shock. Mother was on the couch sewing little silver tassels onto a tablecloth, while Ava and Ana were at her feet making paper roses. Richie watched a few feet away, still keeping an eye on Mother like she was a sheep he was guarding. I touched my face, remembering my cousin's nails in my flesh. Everyone was so busy they barely looked up to see the stupid smock Adele gave me to wear or the patchwork on my face. I hurried to my room and changed into my nightgown, then wrote a hasty note to Winston and returned to the parlor and waved across the room to catch Richie's attention.

"Yes, Cousin Lita?"

"Go to the bar and give this note to Winston. Tell him I've gone to bed."

He hurried off to deliver the message. I imagined him drowning his sorrow in a glass of cheap beer. He needed to go home. Seeing me the day before the wedding would just bring more bad luck, and we didn't need any more bad luck.

Adele opened the door and slipped into the room without knocking. In her hand she had a bowl of something that looked like green mush. "Sit up, girl," she said. "Don't think you going to bed looking like that the day before your wedding."

Adele sat next to me on the bed and reached over and peeled the gauze gently from my face.

"What's that?" I said, pointing to the bowl of green as she scooped a little on the tips of her fingers and spread it onto the dried blood on my cheeks. I winced. Whatever it was, it stung.

"Don't you worry. It's just greens and whiskey. Lucien showed me how to use it. You won't scar, and it'll help you heal."

"Lucien's some kind of doctor?"

"You know he used to work for boxers, stitching their brows and eyelids. I saw him do it. He's some good."

When she finished applying the green stuff, she put

on more gauze. "Your curlers are so loose they won't do a thing." Adele yanked the curlers from my hair and reached into her bag for her own. Her curlers were huge and impossible to sleep on. She rolled her eyes. "Don't start complaining about my curlers hurting your head."

She took her time and put each curler into my hair as tightly as she could. Even though it hurt, I was glad to feel her hands in my hair.

"Your dress is fine. I ironed the hem, but it's fine."

"Good," I said.

"I'm waking you early to get you ready."

"Fine," I said.

"You've got to look good for the both of us," she said, as she departed the bedroom.

Adele was happy. She lived like it didn't matter what happened to her as long as something happened.

Daddy woke me before dawn. I expected the hysterics. He shouted through the door for me to open it, but he could wait for hell to freeze over. Then I thought better about it and put on my robe and unlocked and opened the door to see Daddy's eyes blood-red from drinking, face swollen probably from sleeping facedown on the floor behind the bar.

"What did you and Adele do to my car!"

"It wasn't us, Daddy. It was Aunt Dot. She tried to kill us over thirty dollars. She smashed up your car."

Daddy was in for a world of trouble if he went over there.

"That bitch! She's going to pay me! I'm going there right now and set that cow straight!" Daddy stumbled to the door and grunted good-bye.

He was a dead man.

I sat down on my bed and started painting my nails. Soon as Mother awoke, she'd drag me around, getting me ready like I was her favorite doll. Then I imagined poor Daddy, all rack and ruin, getting the beating of a lifetime from Aunt Dot and her brood. I really didn't want him to die on my wedding day. I rushed out of my room to stop him, and found him on the front steps, nursing a pint and watching the sun come up.

"I thought you were going over Aunt Dot's."

Daddy grumbled. "I might be drunk but I ain't crazy. Let your mother handle that. That's her blood," Daddy said, wisely. "This is your big day," he added, as though he just remembered that fact. "Well, I'd better get myself together. You know, daughters don't get married every day."

"Yes, that's true."

Daddy rummaged around in his pocket until he found his money clip. Fumbling, he slipped off a number of twenties, bills falling from his hand and all over the place as he tried to gather them up.

"Here," he said, and pushed the bills in my direction. "That's your wedding present. Enjoy."

I grabbed hold of the bills and went inside. Funny, even when Daddy was being generous, he made me feel cheap.

The wedding went as smoothly as I could have hoped. Daddy seemed to think it was more of his day to shine than mine. Not only did he act like a perfect husband to his ill wife, he hammed it up so much that even Mother started to look uncomfortable, the way he gingerly led her around like she was about to drop dead at any moment.

Daddy made sure that fresh white roses were all about the church. He also found a woman opera singer to do "Ave Maria," which surprised me; she sang beautifully. I don't know what I expected, but I didn't think Daddy knew anything about music. He was probably trying to get in good with a better class of tramp.

Saint Katherine's overflowed with wedding guests: lots of classmates from Xavier came, probably to see if the wedding was anything to be jealous about. The veil and makeup concealed where Aunt Dot had Sonny jump up on me like some damn tiger, scratching my face like he wanted to gouge another Mississippi into my cheeks. Aunt Dot was crazy and vicious, but regardless, she had done a great job. The wedding dress fit wonderfully, so I guess it was almost worth getting disfigured. I wasn't surprised when she came with her brood of little monsters and her sad-sack husband. She waved and blew kisses like nothing had happened the night before. I figured she'd steal a wedding present or try to devour everything at the reception table to make up for the thirty dollars she thought she was owed.

Daddy led me down the aisle to Winston, and when I saw his reaction I felt like a princess. He stood at the altar with his mouth hanging open, and he didn't think of closing it until Father Fitzpatrick asked for the ring. Having him under my spell, seeing him like a nervous boy waiting to unwrap his Christmas present, made me giddy. That's how a man should be, grateful to be in a woman's presence. Sometimes Winston seemed like he knew everything because he was so much older than me, but as long as I had him bewitched, he'd be mine. He'd listen and treat me with the respect that Mother never got from Daddy, because I knew better. Daddy never looked at Mother that way, like he worshiped the ground she walked on.

Winston slipped the ring onto my finger, and we were pronounced Mr. and Mrs. Winston Michaels, and as we returned down the aisle I tried to keep my eyes straight ahead but couldn't help catching glimpses of the crowd. I saw Daddy's gambling buddies sitting in the pews behind the family. Had to be more than two dozen of them, looking out of place in a church as a bucket of rotting fish, but later at the reception they handed me a derby stuffed with cash.

"Oh yah, we got to do right by Doc's girl," the tiny,

169

dried-up man I saw at the gambling house said as he handed me the hat.

"Got five hun'ed dollars in there," he said before giving me a whiskey-scented wet kiss on the cheek.

Turns out the hat held a little over a hundred dollars, but the money was well used, because the little apartment on Hope Street Winston had found for us needed furniture, and the money would just about pay for most of it. After the wedding, Daddy escorted us to the Cadillac he had borrowed from one of the gambling buddies. "JUST MARRIED" in shaving cream covered the windows, and tails of cans were tied to the bumper. I hadn't seen the barroom since late last night, but now it was even more decked out with wedding decorations. Somebody had even washed the walls so well they looked freshly painted. White crepe-paper streamers hung across the ceiling, and fresh flowers, roses and tulips, were on every table.

"Got them down on the docks. Whole mess of flowers, bought the whole crate. Gonna sell some too. Tomorrow before they dry out. Just gotta get some kids who'll work cheap," Daddy said to Winston as we stood in the receiving line.

Then through all that commotion I saw Rene beaming like he had just won the World Series, arms around Adele, kissing her like he would never let her go. Back together, with all of that evil behind them. They could make it; I truly believed that. Adele was free of Lucien; there was no reason they couldn't get on with their lives. Pretend all of that nonsense never happened. The wedding was a sign. Everything was going to work out for the best. Adele was a saved woman. Anybody could see that.

We honeymooned in the apartment Winston found for us on Hope Street, and even though the lights weren't on yet, we still had a cold bottle of champagne. Winston had some candles, so our wedding night was perfect. I picked out the bed, and it was the only new furnishing we had, but a big bed was a luxury for me and I know it was for Winston too, because since he had been home from the war he had been bunking with relatives, trying to get on with the post office, working back-to-back shifts, sometimes eighteen hours at a stretch. Now all that had changed. We had a very big bed, and I wanted a baby soon as possible. I wanted our baby on the way that first night. In the back of my mind I figured if Mother wasn't long for this life, at least I could have someone there, not so much to take her place but to hold it. I imagined having a little girl enough like Mother that Mother's loss wouldn't be unbearable.

I guess God knows, but keeps us waiting. My prayers were answered, and Mother was there at the hospital when Winston Junior was born.

What I remember about that day is pain. Labor

was the wrong word for what I went through. Blinding and burning agony was more like it. Mother gripped my hand so hard I forgot about the contractions for a minute.

"Don't you go screaming. Don't embarrass yourself," she said, in a harsh whisper.

I told her to go to hell.

I had the baby the following morning. When I did, Mother screamed with happiness, while I screamed in pain.

The baby finally gave up hope of keeping my womb a permanent home, and when he came, fighting and sputtering, Mother shouted, "It's infant Jesus. Oh yes, Lord. That baby's beautiful and perfect as Jesus Christ."

Mother's eyes saw him first, but when I glanced at my son, spotted with blood and whatever else, I couldn't think clearly about anything except for wanting to hold him and to sleep for days. The nurse cleaned my baby and handed him over wrapped like an angelic mummy. Soon as I had him in my arms I knew exactly what Mother meant; blue-eyed, sandy blond hair, sharp features. He looked very much like the paintings of Jesus.

Jesus as white as the whitest white man, just like my little baby boy no one could think of as anything other than white, white like Jesus. What did it mean for colored people to be able to do that, to make a beautiful white baby, prettier than white babies? It was magic. White magic that worked if you believed in the power of whiteness, like it was something to achieve. So we achieved it—Winston and I made one of those babies—and I can't say I wasn't proud that he was beautiful. He was beautiful and he was colored. Colored with us, and when he would be with them, he'd be white for all they'd know. They'd never know he had a Negro heart. They wouldn't have anything on him.

Turns out having the baby was tough on me. Dr. Segrey thought I might not make it through and told Winston he might have to choose between the baby and me. "We are a two-for-one deal," I said. It didn't come to that, but he said I'd have to stay at the hospital for a week to recover.

When Winston wasn't at work he stayed in my room, sleeping in a chair close to my bed, fretting about me, admiring his sleeping son. Mother and Daddy came to visit, but Daddy wasn't happy. It was easy to see from the scowl he wore. He held onto a vase of flowers that I suppose were for me but he couldn't bring himself to part with. Mother took Winnie into her arms, cooing and singing to him.

"What's wrong, Daddy? What did I do this time?"

It was the opening he had been waiting for.

"I can't believe after all I've done for you, you name my first grandson Winston Jr.!"

"Daddy, that's his father's name."

"I don't care. You just don't have respect. I'm your father, Lita. That ought to count for something."

I shook my head, not believing what I heard.

"Adele ain't having a boy. I told your mother that, but she don't believe me. All you got to do is look at how low she's showing."

"Adele's pregnant?"

Daddy laughed. "Open your eyes. Skinny as she is, it's easy to tell."

"Rene's happy as a lark. He can't wait for the baby," Mother said.

"Why didn't she tell me?"

Mother sighed, "Don't you go getting upset. Adele didn't want to steal your thunder. Winnie's here first. She said you deserved your own day in the sun."

"That sounds good, but I don't think I believe it. I think she's just back to her games of trying to drive me crazy."

"There you go trying to run down your sister. You got to get off that kick," Daddy said. He started to light a cigarette.

"Daddy, don't you smoke in here," I said, but he ignored me and lit the cigarette.

Winnie began to cry at the smell, a sad little whine. I'm glad Daddy hadn't given me the flowers. I would have thrown the vase at him.

I wanted to go home with my baby, but one thing after another kept me in that drab, musty room at the hospital. Finally, when I thought I could check out, the doctor wanted to keep me a few more days because he was worried about toxicity. At first I thought he was just being a pain in the ass, but then Winnie couldn't take my milk, and they had to put him on the bottle.

"It's your blood chemistry," Dr. Segrey explained. "We'll try antibiotics and see if we can get you out of here." He was very handsome, dark brown and with features like someone from India. "Don't you worry, Lita. I'll have you out of here soon enough, but I don't think we should rush it. We need to keep an eye on that little one, and we'll be out of the woods."

I nodded, reassured.

Winston did not like him or his bedside manner one bit. "You need another doctor. I don't trust this guy," Winston said, having rushed over to the hospital after a twelve-hour shift at the post office.

"He's a good doctor. He listens to me, and he doesn't talk down to me." Winston rolled his eyes. "You need to go home and get some rest."

"You think I'm jealous?"

"I didn't say one word about you being jealous."

"But you think that, right?"

I shook my head. He was treading on my last nerve.

Just then Adele and Rene appeared in the doorway. Their first visit. I guess I looked so happy to
see them that Winston edged over to the door
and greeted them with grunts. Then Dr. Segrey
returned, and Winston gave up the ghost and barked a
good-bye and disappeared down the hospital corridor.

"Hi there, little man," Adele said, and scooped up
the baby from my arms. Rene leaned over to get a better look at the child.

He stared just a moment too long, and I knew what
he was up to, comparing whiteness. White as Rene
looked, Winnie looked whiter. I don't know if he liked
it or not, and I wanted not to care but I couldn't. I
didn't want him thinking about my baby at all in that
way. Winnie wasn't going to have people talking about
him like I was.

Bad enough some people call me a high yellow nig-
ger or poor white trash; I didn't want that for my boy.
If I had to, I'd move to where no one had ever heard of
Creoles. Maybe out to Los Angeles, where they didn't
have race problems like in New Orleans.

Adele noticed my sour expression. "Rene, you go
get us some po' boys. I'm sure these nurses aren't feeding Lita well."

I nodded eagerly. I hadn't had anything good to eat
since Mother left a chicken sandwich. "You'll have to
sneak them in here. These nurses are strict."

Rene winked, and I noticed his blue eyes. "Don't
you worry. I'll bring Cokes too," he said.

Adele watched him walk down the corridor before she turned to me.

"You're pregnant!" I said.

"Yes," Adele said, and it seemed like some of the wind left her sails.

"What's wrong?" I asked.

Adele sank even further. "I'm lost," is all she could manage to say, as I held her hand and tried to calm her.

"What? What is it?" I asked, and little Winston began crying.

"I'm sorry. I didn't mean to make him cry. He's such a beautiful boy."

"What's wrong, Adele? Don't you change the subject."

"Nothing's wrong. Just things have been rocky lately."

"You and Rene fighting?"

"No, we've been getting along great. He's always tried to make me happy, and now he's going overboard to do that. But it's got nothing to do with him."

"What, then?"

"Lucien."

"Lucien? Is he back?"

I sat there staring at her, waiting for an answer.

"Yes," she said, in almost a whisper.

"Rene'll handle it, and I've got a friend, a cop, Joe La Piccolo. He can help you. He'll make it clear to Lucien what'll happen if he comes around you again."

Adele shook her head, and I knew. She let the devil in through the front door.

"You've been seeing him?"

Adele nodded yes and threw herself across the bed, sobbing, onto my knees. "The baby I'm carrying, it's not Rene's."

"God, no."

178

Funny, her crying seemed to calm Winnie. He nuzzled deeper into my bosom, dozing contentedly.

"How did it happen? How'd you let yourself fall for some nonsense like that? What did Lucien do—shower you with flowers and chocolates when Rene was out of town?"

"I don't know," she said, burying her face, crying into the harsh wool blanket.

"Tell Rene."

"No."

"You have to."

She looked up at me, mascara running down from her eyes, just a mess. "Lucien would kill him. He told me."

"You believe him?"

Adele didn't bother with an answer. I don't know why I asked that question. He would do it. Without a doubt, he'd kill Rene.

"I don't know what to do."

"God, Adele."

"He says if I don't come back to him, I'm going to pay. He's not joking."

"What do you think he'll do?"

"Hurt me."

"Adele, you're carrying his baby. He can't hurt you."

Adele slowly shook her head, then she smiled brightly. "Lucien doesn't care about any of that. If I don't do what he wants, he'll hurt me or worse."

"Why did you see him again? He was out of your hair."

"He was in jail in Miami. I was supposed to bail him out, but I just ran. They didn't have him on anything. I thought he'd get out any day, so I took the money from his bank account to bail him out and went to Los Angeles and stayed with girlfriends. I thought I could start over. Rene would be better off without me, find someone to treat him right, and with me away I hoped Lucien would leave you all alone, but I couldn't do it. I really tried, but I couldn't be away from all of you."

"So, soon as he got out he came looking for you?"

"Oh, yes. Came right to the house and knocked on the door. Thank God, Rene was sleeping. Right there in the living room with Rene sleeping ten feet away, he had me against the wall, kissing me so hard I was sure Rene would wake, and he was choking me till I just about blacked out, and when I got my wits about me he was ripping off my panties and he was in me and when he was done he said to me, Come see me or I'll be back here for more. So I did."

Sighing, Adele sat up and wiped her face and opened her purse and, squinting into a compact, redid her makeup. I tried to think of a plan. Adele had to go, that's it. She just needed to go far away—Los Angeles, Philadelphia, somewhere—stay away.

Rene returned with the sandwiches. Adele smiled brightly, totally composed—she should have been an actress. But no actress could maintain her cool under all that pressure. I don't know if Rene saw it, but Adele had started to shake slightly like she was trying to fight off a chill.

"Goddamn! What's wrong with you two? You're supposed to be planning a baby shower, not a funeral."

We both laughed. Usually I thought Rene was a little slow on the uptake, but he nailed it right on the head this time.

"We better go," Adele said, and after Rene handed me my sandwich, she kissed me good-bye and whispered something to me.

"Pray for me," she said, and kissed the sleeping little Winston.

I watched them leave—Adele walking with shoulders slumped, resigned to whatever her fate might be.

I pulled myself out of bed to call Joe and tell him everything. Something had to be done about Lucien, even if Daddy had to pay Joe to find someone to do it. The walk took a lot out of me, and I barely could make it to the phone by the nurse's station. I dialed the police station and left a message and tried to head back to bed, but weakness reached down to my toes and back up again and I found myself slipping to the cold gray linoleum. I struggled to stand, but no matter how hard I tried, I couldn't get my legs under me. I lay there gasping, trying but unable to catch my breath. Everything started spinning faster and faster until I thought I would vomit. Then I passed out.

*L*ita! Wake up!"

Trying to sleep, and some idiot decides to blind me.

"Lita!"

"What!"

"She's awake."

"Blood pressure?"

"Sixty over forty."

I don't know who decided to have a damn party, but my head is exploding and my little boy needs to sleep, and Mother's still sick. Daddy needs to take his lowlife friends elsewhere.

"She's gone again!"

"Stand back."

"Lita! Goddamn it! Wake up!"

Somebody slapped me!

"Hey! Who the hell do you think you are!" I squinted into the light, but I couldn't see a thing.

"You've got to stay awake. Don't drift away!"

Again! Whoever it was slapped me again.

"Don't you do that!"

I rolled onto my side to get that light out of my eyes. I didn't want to fight, I just wanted to go back to sleep. Then I felt myself being yanked up right.

Again!

"Okay, you SOB!"

I swung hard as I could and felt my fist smash somebody's nose and that damn light crash to the ground and explode.

I saw Dr. Segrey rubbing his nose, and a nurse next to him laughing hysterically.

*H*ome at last, but not my new home. Mother insisted I return with her for the first week of convalescence. She wanted to make sure she could care for me and the baby correctly. I do have to admit Winston was pretty upset. He had made arrangements for his mother, Mrs. Eugenia, to come out from Florida for the same reason, but she was reluctant to move to New Orleans and took her own sweet time in getting here. And the way that Winston talked up his mother, I suspected her arrival wasn't going to make my life any easier.

$\mathcal{M}$*other spent* almost every free morning away from the bar with me and the baby, and Ana and Ava and Richie waited on us hand and foot. It took some getting used to, the family worrying about my comfort. Even Daddy checked in to see how we were making out, but I figured he had an angle.

Mother was obvious about what she wanted to do. Throughout the day she'd appear to hold the baby. Such a look on her face of happiness. But just when I thought Mother had nothing more on her mind than her only grandson snuggling to sleep in her arms, she surprised me.

"For a while there I believed I was going to outlive you with a bad heart and all. You know things like that shouldn't ought to happen. It's not the way God intended." Mother shook her head and held the baby close to her heart.

"Imagine having to raise this little one," she said. "I'm just glad the Lord saw fit for you to stay down here with us."

"I am too," I said.

"Imagine giving birth to such a beautiful baby and having to leave him," Mother said, shuddering.

"Don't think about it," I said.

"You think I don't try?"

The next night I got the phone call from Rene asking for Adele.

"Well, she's supposed to be there," he said. "She said she was going to drop by for a quick visit four hours ago."

Mother took the phone.

"Not a sign of her. If I see her, I'll have her call you," she said, and hung up. Mother looked at me blank-faced. Maybe wanting me to react for her because she wouldn't allow herself to.

"You need to rest," she said, and carried little Winston into the kitchen.

I did need the rest, but I knew I couldn't. What I needed was word on Adele. I needed to hear that she was okay. I needed to hear that she was buying up all the clothes she could get her hands on now that she was back with Rene. Thinking of Adele spending buckets of money put my mind at ease long enough to fall asleep.

Sometime later, I was startled awake by the ringing of the phone.

"Hello?"

I heard Rene's panicked voice.

"Adele? No, but I've been sleeping. I'll check with Mother."

Before I could get out of bed, Mother appeared in the doorway, hands on hips, waiting for the news.

"Adele's still not home?" Mother shook her head,

and she sat down on the corner of the bed and turned away from me. "Call your husband. You tell him to get over here. Then you call around for your Daddy. Tell him to start looking in all the places she might be."

I made the calls and said what needed to be said, but the entire time I thought the worst. Mother handed me a squirming, crying little Winston and left the room but returned quickly, changed from bed clothes into her work dress.

185

"What are you doing? You're not going out?"

"I'm going to the bar."

She left me as fast as she could.

I nursed the baby and tried not to let fear run away with me, but it already had.

*W*e *looked for her.* God, did we look for her. Daddy got the drunks off the bar stools by telling them they could expect a pint or two for any scrap of information. Cousin Harold called up relatives from the country to do their part walking through neighborhoods showing Adele's picture to anybody who wanted to look. Father Fitzpatrick mentioned it at the end of mass. And all those vultures got to mumbling and muttering, "Who's Adele? Oh, that tramp. She's in trouble?" But not a word on her whereabouts.

I went home with Winston. With everybody going in and out looking for Adele it was just like a wake, and

I couldn't stand it. No, it was more like a wake for somebody who had long been expected to die, where everybody is more interested in loading up their dinner plate than grieving or saying a prayer for the dead. Even Daddy lost whatever urgency he had at first, spending most of his time on the porch, drinking and laughing with a few of his gambling buddies. I heard the new whisperings—"Oh, Adele's probably off with another man." It didn't bother me much, but poor Rene, he knew the truth. It wasn't a man's arms she had run to this time.

Mother just shut her mouth and took care of business.

I remember us standing outside on the porch, waving good-bye to some country cousins from across the lake. She watched them drive off, and she spat into her hands and rubbed them together like she was washing them. "Quite a show, eh?"

"What?"

Mother shrugged. "I was never one for pretending. What we need to be doing is getting ready for it."

What nobody had tried to do was find Lucien and make him talk. Adele might have vanished, but he was still among the living. Joe went looking for him, but he

said the trail was cold. Then I'd hear word that someone saw Lucien on the streetcar or at the beach or
across the lake, but Adele wasn't with him. At this
point I would have shot him myself if I had the chance.
Friday evening I had gotten some shrimp for dinner,
but it turned out Winston had another double shift.
The phone rang. Strange, how since then I associate
something like shrimp with bad news, but I do. Never
had a taste for shrimp again. Somehow, I felt that if
maybe the shrimp would have been fresher, the news
would have been different. Maybe they would have
found Adele on dry land and not at the bottom of the
muddy Mississippi, stuffed into a trunk.

Got the call from Mother. She was as calm as I was
hysterical and waited for me get hold of myself.
Between my racking sobs she slipped in marching
orders. "Lita, you need to get to the morgue. Father
Fitzpatrick says the chaplain is having a service for
Adele today at four."

She hung up. It was on me to go. It was her way of
saying you have no choice, this must be done.

Not this time. I wanted to remember Adele alive,
not some corpse covered in pancake makeup. Plus, I
had the baby. I didn't want to drag him out into the
streets to something so sad. It wouldn't be right.

Then Winston came home from work, exhausted
as usual. He dropped into the rocking chair after kissing the baby. Took him long enough to notice me crying onto the potato salad.

"What's wrong, Lita? You upset!"

"They found Adele in the river."

Winston exhaled. He shook his head and forced himself out of the rocking chair to hold me. Not having to mind the baby, I cut loose. It was just a mess. Winston looked shocked and overwhelmed at my grief. All he could do was walk the baby around the apartment, cooing to him as I thrashed about on the bed screaming and sobbing at the top of my lungs.

An hour at least had passed before I could sit upright in control of myself.

I needed to wash my face, and I could hear the baby crying for me, but I wasn't ready to nurse. Just a few more minutes to get myself together.

Then I saw Winston stick his head around the door. "He needs to be changed."

Red anger flashed, and the lamp near the bed flew like an arrow and exploded above Winston's head, showering him and the baby with bits of plaster.

I snatched the baby from his arms, brushed the plaster dust from his hair, and smothered his cries with kisses.

"Sorry! I'm sorry I threw that," I said, without looking at him.

Winston didn't say anything. Think he would have figured out how to change a diaper after watching me do every single one of them. Least he should have tried, being that my goddamn sister was found in the river down there with the catfish and the crabs.

"Listen! I've got to go to the morgue. There's a service for Adele, and I'm going."

Winston threw his arms up. "You just heard they found her and now they're burying her?"

I wanted to fling another lamp at him but none were near, and we had too few as it was. "Mother didn't explain it, but after lying around at the bottom of a damn river for God knows how long, they want to get you in the ground quickly."

Winston walked over to the door and blocked it with his body. "I don't care if you want to be a smart aleck, but I don't want you involved in all this craziness. Somebody killed her and they're still around and I'm not letting you out of here. There's nothing you can do. I'm not letting you go!"

I tried to calm myself. I didn't want to lose it, but he wasn't helping. "This is my sister you're talking about. Please get out of my way."

He wasn't moving. He just shook his head and spread his legs like he was at parade rest. I carried the screaming, red-faced baby into the bedroom and put him down into his crib and dressed for my sister's funeral. I found a black skirt and sweater and a pair of dark blue heels but I had to make do with a light blue blouse. It took a while, but I found a black scarf and I was ready to go. Little Winston had cried himself to sleep, and I was grateful for that. Then I walked back to the kitchen and grabbed the new skillet off the stove and returned to the living room.

189

"Get out of my way or I'm going to smash you in the head with this skillet."

"I don't believe you," Winston said. He stood there with his legs spread and his hands behind his back and his head bowed.

"Winston, I'm telling you, get out of my way."

"No," he said.

190

"I'm telling you," I said, leaning back to throw the skillet. I hoped he wouldn't test me, not this time.

Winston ducked, covering his head with his arms. "Lita, you're crazy!"

But I was already by him. Outside, I left the frying pan by the door and headed down the stairwell to the street.

I got to the morgue with ten minutes to spare. When I finally found someone to direct me to the service, I had only three minutes to get down the stairs to the basement. I ran as fast as I could with heels on to the basement morgue. Even before the last flight of stairs I smelled it. Goddamn, it reeked like the days after someone poisoned all the dogs in the neighborhood and the men piled them up to burn them but it rained and the men went home and forgot about it. The dogs sat there in all that heat and humidity, festering and rotting until somebody got the gumption to drum up some kerosene and a match.

I held my breath and walked through the thick double doors. It wasn't much of a place for a service, just concrete walls and floors, heating ducts and pipes. Along the walls were the refrigerators, big beige boxes with handles that made them look more like filing cabinets for cold paperwork than where they stored dead bodies.

Then I saw the priest setting up chairs by the coffin. It just took a minute to see he was a grade A character: drunk as a pissy skunk and not even able to finish unfolding chairs.

I walked over, happy to be able to do something useful. I nodded to him and started working with the chairs. He watched me work, but then I thought about how Adele hated funerals, and grief hit me like a hurricane. Tears burst from my eyes, and I couldn't see what I was doing.

I sat down in one of the chairs and covered my face with my hands and cried as hard as earlier. Only thing I hoped for was for him to leave me be. I didn't want words of comfort. Get on with it. Get on with eulogizing someone you didn't know.

"Miss," I heard the priest say.

"Yes," I said, struggling mightily to block my river of tears.

"Is there friends or family coming?"

Couldn't this stupid priest see that I wasn't in the mood to be messed with?

"I don't know. I'm here."

The priest shrugged. "Well, I guess we should get started."

I sat right in front of him as he began the mass for one.

As the priest worked his way through the service, I realized Mother wanted me there alone, sharing my grief with no one.

The coffin was plain, the kind they buried paupers in. As I knelt and tried to concentrate enough to pray, I saw a droplet of water hanging from the bottom of the casket and then one more bead along the length of the sideboard, falling to the bare, raw concrete floor. The drops kept coming, one after the other.

Mother wanted me to come to see for myself what Lucien had done.

Drowned like a bag of cats, down there so long at the bottom of the river, she was waterlogged, bloated like a sponge, bleeding water.

The priest finished muttering in Latin and turned to me, hands outstretched. "Go in peace," he said.

Now, no longer performing, he nodded good-bye and slipped away. I was happy to see him go.

I sat there awhile watching the coffin, thankful for privacy, wondering what to do next. What I wanted to do was drag her home with me. Find some way, somehow to get her home. Then I stood and walked slowly to the coffin, wondering what I would do when I got there. It took a minute before I found the courage to run my hands against knotty, rough wood. Then I put my ear to the coffin and heard the soft pinging of the river water falling to the floor.

I wanted to pry the coffin open. I wanted to see her beautiful face, even though now it had to look more like a bloated piece of meat. If I looked at what was left of her, maybe I could understand Lucien. Help me understand the man I hated more than I loved my own child.

193

I drove to Mother's so stunned I couldn't even cry. The house was black. I parked and ran to the door. I didn't care if they were asleep, they'd be awake when I got through shouting loud enough to wake the dead. Up there on the dark porch I tried my key, but I was too hopped up to make it work then I pounded the door and shouted for Mother.

I glanced over to the bar, dark and closed too.

A figure of a man appeared at the edge of the street, and though I was in darkness, he seemed to see me and made a beeline for where I stood.

Not wanting to be trapped on the broad porch, I ran toward whoever it was, which for whatever reason slowed him. I turned quickly, losing my heels, and ran into the night.

After running till my feet ached, I found my way back to the house, clutching my hairpin, expecting the worst. From down the street I saw Ava talking to a policeman, and I thanked God for that much. She shouted and leaped into my arms, and just then Winston came up, driving like a lunatic. He burst from the car, but I told him I was alright. After checking on little Winnie sleeping in the backseat, I hurried back to the policeman.

He shook his head. "Can't get this one to talk."

"Is everyone okay?" Winston asked as he handed the baby to me. He hurried into the house to see for himself.

The cop nodded. "We need to know what happened here. Your mother isn't up to talking. All we got to go on is these two girls."

I set Ava down on the steps and rubbed her back until she was calm enough to talk. Once I got her going, she turned her face from me and began speaking quickly, as if the memories couldn't wait to tumble from her mouth.

In the pitch-black kitchen we watched the blue flame make the big gallon pot boil. Ana held onto Mother's leg like she didn't need it to walk. Mother made us run into the kitchen like the devil was chasing us when the lights went out.

"I'm scared," Ana said, and Mother picked her up and whispered loud enough for me to hear. "Be quiet. Don't say another word."

Ana crawled under the table over to me and we locked our arms together. She was shaking scared. I felt the hot water dribbling down her leg but I didn't say nothing.

I watched the blue fire under the pot, hoping for Daddy to come home. We were scared because Mother was scared. We never saw Mother scared before but she was. She didn't tell us but we heard about that bad man killing Adele and now he had done something to Daddy. Mother hung up the phone, cursing about it not working, and put that big pot of water on and made us sit under the table and told us not to say a word. Richie wouldn't get under the table. He followed after Mother. Mother mumbled to herself 'bout how she needed something but Daddy took it. I always found Mother's glasses, her purse, scissors, whatever she needed but I couldn't ask her what she was looking for. Mother wanted us quiet and she looked at us like she do when she really mad. Mother tried to hide a big knife in her apron pocket. She circled around the kitchen listening hard for something and every now and then moving the heavy curtain covering the window and peeking out and then leaning away like somebody might have seen her.

Mother had locked both doors in the kitchen. I was wishing Daddy would be coming by to turn on the lights and help us but thinking about Daddy made me feel worse than scared. I started to cry and Mother walked over to me and squatted down and grabbed my face in her hands.

"Ava!" she said. "I don't expect this from you!"

I stopped crying. Mother could make my tears stop and run back up my eyes.

"I need you to listen, keep listening for trouble. That's what I need you to do."

Then we heard the pounding on the front door.

"It's Daddy," Ana shouted, and Mother slapped her so hard she fell into my lap. "You be quiet!"

The noise kept up and I wet myself too. Sounded like the door was gonna break into little pieces.

Then it stopped.

After a long time Mother stood up, walked to the window, and looked out. Then like something bit her she jumped back, almost falling.

"It's him!" she said.

"Is he gonna get in?"

Mother didn't have time to cuff me upside the head. She was too busy slipping on pot holders, then she made us all stand against the wall.

"Listen," she said. "He can't get into the house without a whole lot of trouble. But if he does, I'm gonna throw this on him. Then I want you to run out the front door and keep going."

Ana looked at me and squeezed my hand so hard it hurt. Richie nodded his head.

Then I heard something. A scraping. Like something being dragged. It was coming from beneath the house. Mother heard it too.

"That's how he does it," she said.

Then we heard muffled chopping and Ana started to scream and I did too. Mother grabbed that big pot of steaming hot water and stood over where the chopping seemed to be coming from.

Then the floorboard splintered and I saw a claw rip through the wood beneath the floor and that's when we saw hands and a man pulling himself up into the kitchen.

Mother poured the pot of hot water on him and that man screamed like a hurricane horn and dropped back down below the house.

Mother knocked all of the plates and the sugar pot and salt and pepper shakers off the table and waved us over.

"Help me turn this over!" she ordered.

It took a minute, but we flipped that heavy old oak table. It landed with a thud, then Mother grabbed the legs and pulled it on top of the chopped-through hole in the floor.

"Got that bastard good," Mother said. "He won't be coming back tonight."

Mother unlatched the door leading to her bedroom and it was easy to see she was sick again. Her bed was right there but she couldn't make it. Mother slid to her knees and barely could crawl to the wall where she pulled herself up.

I took a pillow off her bed and put it behind her head and Richie put one under her feet.

Then I went to go get help and ran right into a chair.

With my head burning I got up and ran some more.

I made it to the parlor holding my forehead feeling a big old knot growing right there.

In the dark I searched for the door handle.

Then I heard steps on the porch and I froze. A flashlight lit up the parlor.

Then I heard the door unlocking, and as it swung open I took off running for the kitchen. Knocked over one chair then another.

The lights came on and upside down I saw Big Winnie and he had a gun in his hand.

I leaned over and looked under the porch and saw two other cops sliding through an opening beneath the house. They took a long time, but they came back looking dusty and with mud on their hands. One policeman had a crowbar and a short ax he found under the house.

"Well," the cop said, who was writing everything down, "your mother got him good. He left all his tools and his cap." He held up the cap to show us. "It's soaked too. Look, you can see his hair. Boiling water poured on your head will do that to you."

"Can you catch him?" Big Winnie asked.

The cop laughed. "We're gonna try."

I returned to the house, feeling sick to my stomach.

I couldn't stand another minute of sweltering like stewed chicken in a Dutch oven in that sweaty little apartment. Lake Pontchartrain rolled into view, all blue and cool like ice in a desert. If I could swim I'd dive headfirst in. The taxi driver was nice, so I gave him a fifty-cent tip and he helped me set up the stroller. I put Winston inside and he slept through the whole thing.

"Come back in a hour and a half," I told the cab driver.

The beach wasn't very crowded, and we rolled by white children playing catch and racing on the lawn, and I was so glad to be there. I headed to the snack bar, past the Whites Only sign. Winston hated for me to go to Pontchartrain, because I wouldn't go to the colored beach if I could avoid it. It's the worst corner of the beach, like we're lepers and the crackers sit pretty feeling like they deserve the best. Winston was always worried about someone seeing me on the beach and telling a supervisor at his job. I understood he didn't want trouble, but you've got to stand up for yourself.

Winnie woke up in time for me to hand him an ice-cream cone, which he wolfed down in a few messy minutes, and after cleaning him up and finding a shady bench I took him out of the stroller to play on the grass.

A pretty white woman with a colored nanny, sitting across from me at a picnic table, had the same idea, playing happily with the little blond girl at her feet. She made a big deal of wiping the child's running nose every few minutes, but I guess I could be that attentive if I had help standing behind the stroller, handing me tissues. She saw me looking at her child and called over to me.

"Lovely day for the beach," she said, and looked longingly at Winnie. "Oh, I did so want a boy, but when Darleen was born we just painted the blue nursery pink and made do."

"Your girl's some pretty."

"And so's your son. Maybe we could set them up. We'd have some of the prettiest grandchildren in this whole, wide world."

"Wouldn't that be great," I said as I struggled to get the handful of grass out of Winston's hand and his mouth. Then after quickly loading Winnie into the stroller, I waved good-bye to the white woman, but her nanny stared me up and down like she knew me and knew that I was colored.

I decided to head back to where the taxi driver said he would meet me. It really wasn't that far, but I hadn't been sleeping well, and my stomach churned like I hadn't eaten in days. I couldn't deny it. This was just how I felt carrying little Winston. I knew I should be happy, but I wasn't ready for another one. Not right now. Little Winston wore me out, and I didn't see how I could handle two children.

The parking lot was at the end of the grove of trees, and I slowed down seeing that Winnie was on the verge of falling back to sleep.

Then I heard his voice. At first I was stopped sharp

by the sound. The "hello" was said in a deep, sweet voice, but it unnerved me like the sound of rats skittering in the pantry. I turned, and there was Lucien. He smiled warmly with that vicious mouth of his, menacing but charming all the same.

"You'd better keep away. I'll scream."

He laughed but kept his distance, taking off his hat and fanning himself. I despised Lucien, but I couldn't ignore how handsome his face was that led Adele to the bottom of the Mississippi. The hair he used to have was gone, and in its place was a reddish splotch. Mother's aim was true, and that bastard would have the mark of a couple gallons of boiling water for the rest of his miserable life.

"Passing's easy for you. You're comfortable around crackers. Why shouldn't you be? You look white. You deserve to have nice things and go nice places."

Lucien's voice was so smooth. He took a step in my direction.

"Stay away. I'll scream rape. People will think you're trying to rape a white woman. I'm not joking. You'll get lynched."

He sighed and took a step backward. "Don't you get alarmed. I'm being sociable."

I looked around to see for passersby, but where we stood, on a path surrounded by a grove of trees, we were alone. I scooped Winnie up from the stroller and thought of running for the parking lot.

"Funny to think about, you know. If you did get

me strung up out here by a bunch of dickless crackers, maybe I'd be the first negro lynched because of the lies of a colored woman passing for white," he said, all the while smirking.

I began inching away, and he didn't try to stop me.

"You Du Champs brought this on yourselves. First of all, you blame me for everything. You act like I'm the root of all evil. You probably don't know how your mother stole someone very important away from me. A woman I loved. It was a long time ago, but I can't forget and forgive. And she got me arrested and I spent years busting rocks. She wronged me, and I needed to set the scales right. And that's what I've done. My quarrel with your family is over. You can tell her that."

"What? You had to kill my sister to make things right?"

Lucien carefully arranged his hat on his head. He was strangely calm, as if I hadn't accused him of killing Adele. It was like he was thinking things over and I just happen to be standing there. "That's neither here or there. I don't know how Adele died. I miss her, I wish she was still with me," he said.

I laid Winnie onto the ground and yanked that stroller into the air and did my best to smash this lying pig upside the head, but he lifted his large forearms and knocked it aside.

"Adele's not your blood. She's no relation to you. Your mother stole her from someone who was important to me. That's why she hates me. Because I know. I know her story."

He tipped his hat and turned around and walked back toward the lake.

I picked up my baby and ran for my life.

He means to kill us all," Mother said, so matter-of-factly she could have been asking me to order another case of beer.

"He didn't say that. He said he was through with us. He's going to leave us alone."

Mother sneered as she poured boiling, soapy water into a big tin bucket.

"Do you want to believe that? Are you hoping it's over and he's done with us? You think because you want something to happen, it's going to happen?"

Mother slipped heavy beer and shot glasses into the still-steaming water without wincing. I never did understand how she could take sticking her hands into scalding water without screaming.

"You need to take your baby out to Aunt Odie in the country. She might be crazy as a June bug, but she'll protect him." Mother paused, sighing. Then she cried, softly, almost tearlessly. "Oh yes! Adele was mine. I saved her mother from ruining both their lives. That baby wouldn't have made it if it wasn't for me. But why are you listening to anything that man had to say? Lucien doesn't deserve to live. What he's done to us, he done to others. I don't know why God lets him live. But I won't. It's not going to be over till he's dead."

"Who's going to do it?" I asked.

Mother snorted. "Call that friend of yours. Tell him to come by, because we need to talk."

"Talk about what? Joe can't find him. What's going to be different?"

Mother shook her head slowly. "You let me to talk to him. I'll handle it."

Later that night there was a knock at the door and Daddy answered it. He flung the door open like he would catch Lucien, but it wasn't Lucien. It was a tall white man in a policeman's uniform. Daddy did something to truly make a fool of himself: he pulled from his waist band a shiny, snub-nosed gun. Joe was stunned to see the gun pointed at him, but I caught Daddy's arm and pulled it down.

"Daddy, you almost shot a cop."

He shrugged and turned away like he hadn't heard a word I said.

"Hi, Joe. Sorry."

He brushed himself off and caught his breath. "Y'all seem pretty damn jumpy around here."

"Lucien's back."

"That rat?"

"Yes, he slipped up on me at the lake, and there wasn't a damn thing I could do."

"You were at the lake? What did you do?"

"I told him I'd yell rape."

"That made him leave you alone?"

"I broke my stroller trying to hit him."

Joe's hands clinched, and his face reddened. I patted him on the back and led him inside to see Mother. She was in the kitchen, putting food on the table for dinner. She didn't smile when she saw Joe; it was all business.

"Sit down," she said.

Joe sat quickly.

"Listen."

"Okay, ma'am." Joe knew he was in for it.

"I've known your father for years, and we've had a good relationship."

"Yes'um," Joe said, sounding more like the frightened boy by the minute.

"So what about this Lucien? A colored man walks around New Orleans killing like a mad dog, and nothing can be done?"

"I've tried to find him."

"He's not a ghost or a bogeyman. He's got to be somewhere."

"I know. But it's just that the police don't—"

Mother turned her head and spat. "I know, the police don't have time to see about colored crime. But I'm not going to stand by and let this man kill any more of my children."

"Mrs. Du Champ, you know I am doing my best. But he don't live in one place. He's got women who do for him. He don't have to lift a finger. And those women don't talk."

"Money talks," Mother said, pulling a fat envelope from her apron pocket. Joe looked at the envelope but didn't pick it up. "There's a hundred dollars in there. I want you to spend this money to find him. Do what you need to."

Joe rubbed his chin.

"I'll pay to have it taken care of. I'll pay a lot to know he's gone." Mother stared at Joe so hard I thought his head would burst into flames.

"I can't take your money. I wouldn't feel right when it's my job and all."

Mother waved him off. "Listen, Joe. Those other cops don't give a fig about Lucien. The only thing some of these crackers understand is cash."

Joe shrugged.

"Money will loosen their tongues, even if they'd just as soon see Negroes shooting each other."

"Yes—" Joe said, but the conversation was over. Joe tried to hand the money back to her one last time, but Mother held her hand up, and he let the idea go.

"Just find him, is all I'm asking you. Now, drop this subject—it's time to eat."

I called the children, and Mother brought fried chops out to the table, and soon as Joe saw them his awkwardness disappeared. If he looked for Lucien a tenth as hard as he devoured those pork chops, he'd find him before sunrise.

I thought I could make it home before Winston and do something about dinner. Lately he was working two back-to-back shifts at the post office, like many of the new colored workers had to do. He'd get home around six in the evening—bone-weary, but he did his best to play with the baby. Then I'd fix him dinner, and after a shower and a very short nap he'd head back to work. But I'd lost track of time at Mother's, and I realized I wouldn't have time to cook something for him so I wrapped a few chops to make sandwiches. Even though he didn't care for sandwiches, it was all I could think of. Then I still had to bird-dog Daddy to get a ride home, and it took forever to pry him away from his buddies getting plastered at the bar.

On the drive home he started whistling, loud and sharp, enough to keep the baby from drifting to sleep.

"Daddy, could you cut that racket out? Winnie can't sleep."

"Babies like my whistling. That's how I got you to sleep."

It was all I could do not to reach over and slap him upside the head. Now I know why I had nightmares as a child. Finally, we arrived at the apartment building.

"I'll watch you get in from here," Daddy said, refusing to leave the comfort of the Packard.

I gathered Winnie and the food and hurried to the stairs. I have to admit I was scared almost out of my wits going up those dark stairs clutching the baby to my chest. I guess I should have been glad Daddy said he would wait for me—it wasn't what I expected from him. When he beeped his horn twice, as if hearing two sharp beeps would cheer me, and took off in a quick U-turn before I had opened the door, I can't say I was surprised. It's what I expected.

The apartment was dark, and I was hopeful Winston hadn't gotten home. I unlocked the door, and then I thought about Lucien, and now I didn't want to walk inside. No, I wouldn't go in. I turned and sat on the hard concrete steps of the apartment, cradling the baby, and prepared to wait for Winston to get home.

"Lita! What are you doing sitting outside?" Winston took the boy from me and looked him over.

"Nothing wrong with him, is there?"

"No, it was just too hot in the house."

"It's not that hot."

"Oh, it's cooled off. But earlier, some hot, yes it was."

Winston led the way into the house, and I watched him fumble for the light switch, all the while still questioning me about the steps. I wanted to yell at him to pay attention, be careful, be something other than a dead man. He managed to flip on the light, and there was no Lucien with a knife in his teeth and a gun in his hand.

"What are you nervous about? Are you coming down with something, do you feel alright?" Winston looked me up and down. One thing about the man is that he believes in going to the doctor at the first sniffle or cough, and he likes to drag everybody else with him too.

"No, I'm okay. Nothing's wrong with me."

"Then why you're acting so strange? What's the problem, soldier?" Lately, he'd taken to calling me "soldier." He liked to think of me as being his little soldier, and I couldn't figure out how to tell him how stupid it sounded without hurting his feelings and getting into a big fight.

209

"Any dinner?" he asked, after looking around the kitchen.

"I brought you some chops from Mother's. I just need to heat them up."

"Okay," he said, with this look of hopelessness on his face. I ruined his whole damn life because I didn't have his dinner ready in time.

I couldn't tell him that I'd seen Lucien in the park, and what Mother was doing about it. Winston couldn't do any more than Rene did trying to protect Adele. If Winston suspected anything at all, he'd run off half-cocked trying to prove his manhood, and it wouldn't do any good. This didn't have anything to do with manhood. This was about survival.

A week passed, but the tension didn't ease, not at all. People started to spot Lucien around town. More than one drunk showed up at the bar saying, "Saw Lucien. He asked 'bout you." If I wanted to know more, I'd have to come across with a free whiskey or two to hear the punch line: "He's coming by the bar soon to give you the good word."

Ha, he was one funny son of a bitch.

Mother heard the rumors too. Lucien, who could fade in and out of lives like a murdering ghost, was now planning for some kind of showdown.

"He's coming. It's going to be over soon now. He wants it to end. He's tired of playing around," Mother said. We were in the kitchen counting the night's money and storing it away in the safe.

"A robbery. He's going to come in late one night after we've thrown out the last bum. Then he'll come in and do his best to shoot us down. That way it'll look like a robbery. And the police will just shrug and close the books and that'll be that."

"Mother, you sound like you know. Did somebody tell you?"

Mother smiled like I just missed the boat. "Your Aunt Odie. She tells fortunes."

Bad enough all the kids were with her, but now she was predicting how I would meet my demise.

"So what are we going to do?"

Mother stood up slowly, looking thin and frail as she gave me a smile that was less than reassuring. "We'll play it by ear," she said as she checked to see if the door was locked.

We did what we could to protect ourselves. Mother hired a retired cop, a cracker by the name of DeLancy, to work nights, but Mother had to threaten not to pay him a dime if he left before we closed up and counted out the bar money. I guess this idiot thought because we were colored we'd let him off work before we bolted the door and turned out the lights. Joe volunteered to come and put his shotgun on the bar, but he never made it. Something always seemed to come up, but Mother didn't complain.

"First thing's going to happen is the guy with the gun is going to get shot," she said, and she didn't want that guy to be somebody doing a favor for the family.

Still, I don't see why she was paying the cracker. The man was steadily drinking. We hardly had to pay him because he ran such a big tab. He was worthless.

We waited for the worst.

Even Daddy made an attempt at watching out for us. He did his drinking on the porch, keeping an eye peeled for Lucien before he passed out drunk. Winston didn't know a thing, and it would stay that way; I didn't need to hear his opinion about my family. He didn't want his own family too close, and he didn't have any great sense of obligation to them. That was fine for him, but that wasn't how I could live. He already wanted to move us out to California, and he'd been bringing it up more often lately.

Mother bought two guns. One she kept in her apron, and the other stayed behind the cash register. I'd never shot a gun. I never even held one except for the time Winston tried to show me how to use his rifle and it misfired. He said it was no big deal, but Daddy told me I was lucky the damned thing didn't explode in my face.

We were always together now. Mother wouldn't let me out of her sight. I spent so much time home with Mother, I might as well been living with her all over again. Winston had a lot to say on the subject when I'd come home to make his dinner.

"I want you back home! And what about my boy? Winnie's been at your Aunt Odie's for weeks."

Winston was at the end of his rope, but I wasn't going to explain the situation to him. It was going to happen soon. I could feel it, like when the big hurricanes were growing out in the Gulf. Pressure drop would make your skin crawl, and you'd know it was going to be a big one if you paid any attention at all.

"I'm home. I'm always home when you're here. I'm helping Mother when you're at work. What's wrong with that?" I said to Winston.

"I like knowing you're here. This is our home. That was your home. You should be here."

Winston's brown eyes would grow dark when he was angry. They looked like burned charcoal.

"Winston, calm yourself. I'm not trying to get away

from you, but you need to understand how much my mother means to me. She needs me and I'm going and nothing's going to change that. Nothing in the whole wide world."

Winston left for work without a backward glance, without the lunch I made for him or offering me a ride to Mother's.

When I wasn't with Mother I felt like something horrible would happen—maybe she'd disappear and we'd find her in a trunk, like Adele at the bottom of the Mississippi. If Mother was right and Lucien was planning something, I had to be there. This was where I had to be. I guess I should feel safe with DeLancy here, but as soused as he was, drinking beer after beer, I doubted he could protect himself, let alone Mother or anybody else.

I worked the bar more than I ever had, waiting to see him, expecting at any moment to see his handsome face and that vicious smile. The barroom full of drunks would pull themselves up from whatever stupor they were in and would instantly know who had walked in and it would be on me. He would sit there in a chair near the door waiting for the drunks to stumble home and then we would be alone and I would see.

This evening was slow, slow enough so that Mother could go to bed early and I could spend too much time thinking about Lucien. Over and over as I opened beers and poured whiskey I saw myself shooting him. *When he comes in, I grab the gun from the drawer beneath the cash register and work my way over to him, and soon as he smiles — or smirks, or makes any move — I shoot every bullet into his thick head.*

214   I saw it first through that dirty, barred window of the door; flames from across the way, just starting to dance and flick the sky. What was burning? After wiping the greasy window, I could see Mrs. Wilson's picket fence burning. Neighborhood kids could do some damned stupid things, but that fence was more or less just firewood, unfit even for the scrap heap, no big loss. I watched for a minute, feeling guilty about enjoying someone else's trouble. The neighbors across the street were yelling and screaming, trying to put out embers that carried to her roof. I watched a man struggling to hose it down and others doing their best to help. I just hoped the fire didn't jump up and send more sparks our way.

"DeLancy, go see about that fire. Turn on that hose."

That fat cracker ignored me. He sat sipping his beer like he had every right to look through me. The bar was empty. I'd have to do it myself. "Listen, I'm locking the door behind me. Don't let anyone in." That asshole just grunted. I turned to go but thought about the gun, slipped it into my apron like Mother would do, and headed outside.

Then the fire erupted, and I thought Mrs. Washington's house had caught. I heard the faint sound of fire sirens, and I ran to the front of the house for the hose. I knew before I got there that it wasn't her house but our house on fire. I saw the door blazing. Someone had to have doused it with kerosene. Lucien! I turned on the hose and wet down my hair and hosed the door, trying to beat back the fire. It was too much. The fire crept up the ceiling of the porch and burned hotter. I gave up and ran back to the bar to get in that way. I hoped Mother had gotten out. I unlocked the door and rushed in, calling for Mother. Already smoke was flooding the bar, but I continued on blindly to Mother's room. I kicked something and almost tripped. DeLancy. I didn't touch him. Blood pooled beneath his body like a dark blanket. Mother's door was pushed open. I tried to stand, but a wave of hot air scorched me. I dropped to my knees and crawled as thick, black smoke flowed through the hallway.

"Mother! It's Lita!"

She was crumpled in the corner, her white nightgown gone almost red with blood. I crawled to her, reaching out as I coughed and gasped for air. Through burning eyes I saw Lucien swatting at the air like a crazed bear. I saw a straight razor in his hand. I reached for the gun.

"Where are you? You little bitch!" he bellowed over the roar of the fire. His smoldering shirt burst into flames at the edges, but still he sliced at the air. I shot. He heard the gun but kept coming anyway. I shot again, and this time I think I caught him. He fell to his knees and I shot again and he turned and crawled to the hallway. I grabbed Mother — her arms were shredded and gashed to the bone — and dragged her away. I knew I would die if I didn't make it to the barroom. I pushed DeLancy aside and crawled along the length of the hall until my elbows and knees were aching. The hall wasn't long, but the heat was unbearable. I detoured to the kitchen. I pushed it open, and there I saw Lucien on the floor, gasping for air. Startled, I dropped the gun, and Lucien lurched for me. His razor came inches from my face.

I recoiled and lunged back out of the room and grabbed the red-hot door handle and slammed it shut. With a surge of panic I clutched Mother and crawled madly down the hallway to the bar, but it too was black with smoke. The door to the backyard! I locked it behind me. I set Mother down and reached for the key, but my hands were so fried I couldn't feel it in my apron. I slumped onto the floor, gasping the burning air.

The door splintered open, and I saw hands and bodies coming toward me. I felt myself being dragged out into frigid air. "Mother!" I yelled.

I saw someone carrying her, and as our rescuers rushed away from the house I heard a scream. A flaming man burst from the burning barroom and ran in desperate, crazed circles as people tried to catch up to him. Finally someone threw a blanket over him and hurled him to the ground and rolled him like a pin until he lay there smoldering and charred, that straight razor still clutched in his hand.

We buried Mother two days later at the Saint Louis Cemetery near to Adele, and with all the responsibilities of arranging it, I didn't have time for grief. Mother had many friends, and everybody pitched in to do her justice. For that day Daddy was inconsolable, crying and carrying on about how he couldn't do without his Helen. And to make sure everybody knew how serious he was about his grief, he hired professional mourners to wail and pull at their hair like madwomen as the pallbearers carried the coffin out of the church. Ava and Ana kept themselves under control, holding hands and crying and staying close to me. Richie wasn't there. Aunt Odie said he took off from her home across the Lake soon after he arrived with the girls. They knew.

"Richie wanted to see about Mother. That's what he talked about. He was going home to protect Mother."

Joe confirmed what I had suspected. Lucien was blinded—that's why he couldn't get out. Mother couldn't explain it from the grave, and neither could Lucien. I knew she fought him, and I hoped she tore his eyes out of his head before she died, but Joe said his face wasn't clawed.

Pregnant as I was, I had Winston drive me over to Aunt Dot's. I had sense enough not to approach the door, knowing she'd attack me like the mad animal she was. I thought she'd still be up to the same tricks, and I was right. Richie was sitting on the porch, I called to him, and he came reluctantly. As he got closer, I could see the boy had been burned. The skin on his face looked badly blistered, and one of his eyes was partially swollen shut. He had more burns on his hands and arms. I turned my head and began weeping. I heard Winston gasp and say, "I'll be damned."

"Open the damn door, Winston. Let him in. We've got to get him to the doctor."

The front door of Aunt Dot's opened. I could see her standing there, staring across at us like it was a big joke. She called to Richie, and he hesitated.

"Get in, Richie." I said. "You're coming to live with us. That's what Mother would have wanted for you."

He got into the car and we drove off. We drove him to Charity Hospital without exchanging a word, until we heard him mumbling.

"What?" I asked.

"I threw that lye because Aunt Helen couldn't reach it because she was trying to fight him off." The boy started crying. "I got scared and I ran off. I left her."

"Richie—you did your best."

"But she died 'cause of me."

"No, that was gonna happen anyway. But you

stopped him. He would have killed me and everybody else if you wouldn't have done what you did."

He bucked up after that. He was a strong boy.

We went to the bar to get Ana and Ava. "Get yourselves ready," I said. "We're leaving for California, and you two are coming."

They nodded their heads in perfect unison, looking more like mirror reflections than two girls who had on different dresses.

"Daddy isn't gonna let us," Ava said.

"How do you know?"

" 'Cause we already asked him."

"We'll see about that," I said.

I told the girls to expect me Saturday, to be dressed and ready to go, and to wait for me on the porch.

I pulled up to the front of the house, and there they were, both carrying pillowcases with their clothes and toys.

I maneuvered my big belly around the steering wheel and lumbered out to help them get situated in the backseat. I wanted to just hop in, but there was hardly space for them to squeeze between the boxes Winston loaded earlier. Then, on cue, the front door swung open, and there was Daddy with a bat in his hand, screaming to high heaven.

"You two get back here! Ava, Ana! Come now, listen to your father!"

I put the station wagon in drive, but Daddy rushed in front of the car, waving the bat like that would stop me.

"Get back, Daddy," I shouted, but he ignored me.

"Give me my girls!"

"No! They need to be in a real home."

Daddy busted one of my headlights. "Get out, or I'm gonna wreck this car good!"

"Mother wants them to come with me!"

"She's dead. Who cares what she wants!"

I turned to the girls in the backseat. They were crying, pulling at their pigtails. I thought of running Daddy over, but not with them in the car.

"Be right back," I said, and I huffed out of the car. Daddy still held the bat above his shoulder like he might come at me, but he stepped backward, giving me space. I still had the keys to his Packard. Oh, did he have that car dolled up since I last saw it—shiny new paint job, bumblebee yellow with new upholstery. I unlocked the door and started the engine and checked the rearview window. The car was directly in front of the new porch and the two beams holding it up. I gunned the engine till it roared. Daddy flung the bat aside and ran screaming for me to stop. I took my foot off the brake and threw the car in reverse.

The car squealed up the wooden stairs, but then I was shooting backward up onto the porch, knocking aside support posts and the porch roof. The car kept going, smashing through the front door into the parlor, through the dining room, stopping only when it slammed against the kitchen wall. I struggled out of the car and looked at the damage I caused. The walls, the ceiling, and the furniture, everything was knocked aside, sagging, or destroyed. The front of the house looked like the entrance to a cave. I started down the hallway to the bar, but then there was Daddy, pulling at his hair and crying. He was so distraught he didn't even see me walk by him and down the hall to Mother's room. I could smell the cheap perfume she used to wear. I stopped at the photograph in the fancy frame on the bureau. The one good photograph of Mother and all of us together, me and Adele and Ava and Ana at the beach. A picnic I couldn't remember—none of us girls looked too happy, but Mother was. I put the photograph under my arm and walked slowly to the station wagon, hearing Daddy crying for his house, his car, everything that truly mattered to him. Everything that mattered to me was loaded up in the station wagon. I didn't look back. There was no need to.

*W*atching *Winnie clean* those damn windows for the fifth time and the fact that we hadn't moved an inch made me nuts. Bad enough to be pregnant on the road, pregnant, traveling with a colicky baby, kidnapped sisters, and an inconsolable cousin, but I've got to be with a man who doesn't understand I want to put miles between me and New Orleans before my water breaks, and we still need to stop at the Saint Louis Cemetery.

Winston sprayed the windshield and wiped like his life depended on it.

"Come on, damn it! Let's get on the road before everybody has to use the bathroom again!"

He rolled his eyes like I had no right to rush him.

"What? You want me to have the baby here?"

He squints like I'm joking.

"You ready? Now?"

The dirty white rag hangs low in his hand. "Lita, sit back. I can have you at the Charity Hospital in ten minutes!"

"Damn it, Winston! I want to get to the cemetery before these flowers wilt, and then I want to get on the highway."

His eyes narrowed, and his shoulders hunched up. Finally he slid behind the wheel and drove off down that narrow street I hoped never to see again.

It took a while to find them among the many vaults along the thick wall. Mother and Adele were interred in the wall vaults that encircled the cemetery; Mother was below Adele, and her vault seemed sunken, as did the other vaults on the bottom row. With the family trailing behind me, Winston held little Winston awkwardly, trying to shield him from the torturous sun; the girls pulled their sun hats low over their eyes, and Richie just squinted. I placed the flowers in front of Mother's vault. Rene must have brought fresh flowers for Adele, because a dozen roses were in front of her vault. Richie put his hands against the marble plaque and cried unrestrainedly. His tears got me to crying, and the girls joined in.

223

"Come in, Lita. This heat is murder," Winston said.

I agreed and led the girls and Richie to the car. We had said our good-byes.

The ride through west Louisiana was miserable as being stuck in a pot full of half-cooked crabs. Little Winnie sat in my lap, sucking listlessly at his thumb, his sweaty skin plastered against me. The girls scuttled about, crawling over each other to get at the window for as much of the breeze as they could stand, and Richie stared straight ahead, so stunned over Mother he didn't even seem to feel the heat.

I never crossed the Texas state line before, and when I saw that sign, You Are Entering the Great State of Texas, I realized I was free of black-hearted Louisiana.

Once Winston got into the groove of driving, he didn't want to stop. He didn't talk much, he just drove. After the first three hundred miles he started whistling, "Oh, when the Saints," and didn't stop for the next hundred miles until I couldn't stand it no more and told him to stop whistling or I'd get out and walk.

He frowned, but he stopped. Then I heard him talking to himself, mumbling about baseball, replaying games in his head he heard on the radio.

When we drove into the lonely twilight of west Texas, I could feel my heart lightening. The girls were asleep, and little Winston dozed, breathing easily in the cooling air. Winston went on and on about how well the roads were marked, unlike "Lousy-ana," and about how much gas this trip would cost, and about how it would be difficult to find a colored motel.

We weren't staying at some fleabag colored motel. We'd either find something decent, or we'd have to sleep in the car all night.

I figured we could do another two hours of driving. The farther we drove, the easier it was for me to think. Adele. Took all of my control not to burst into tears, but Winston heard me sob.

"What's wrong?"

"Nothing," I said.

Up ahead I saw lights; maybe a town, at least a fill-up.

We pulled into another dump of a gas station, just one pump and a sad little garage and snack shop. Winston pulled up through a swarm of the little bugs we had been squashing against the window all through the drive.

"Sodas," I said to Winston. He walked away, shoving his hands deep into his pockets. I thought of Mother and sobbed again so loud I woke the girls and Richie.

"Are we there?" Ava asked.

"No, now you all hush before you wake the baby."

Winston returned with the sodas, handed them through the window, and then, sipping from his soda, attacked the windshield with wads of paper towels and soapy water, like he had been dying to get back to it since we left New Orleans.

"When you finish with your little window, please take the kids to the toilet."

The girls took that as their cue and pulled Winston from that fascinating windshield. I was sure they would get that tightfisted man to spring for more sodas. Richie halfheartedly trailed after them.

Alone with the baby, I could cry to my heart's content. Ava and Ana, I would do whatever I could to protect them, but thank the Lord I didn't have a girl. Seems like no matter how strong a woman is, it's not strong enough.

Winston came back, holding the girls' hands, all of them like they didn't have a care in the world, in contrast to Richie's grim face. "Lita, that grease monkey says there's a colored motel five miles east."

"Hell with that, Winston. You keep driving."

"Keep driving? If we don't find something now, all the motels are gonna close up. We'll have to drive all night."

"That's fine with me. Pull over if you get tired."

"So you want me to drive till daybreak?"

I nodded. "I just want to see the sunrise."